THE ROGUE KNIGHT

MARCIA LYNN McCLURE

Published by Distractions Ink
1290 Mirador Loop N.E.
Rio Rancho, NM 87144

©Copyright 2016 by M. Meyers
A.K.A. Marcia Lynn McClure
Cover Photography by © Bblood/Dreamstime.com
Cover Design and Interior Graphics by Sandy Ann Allred/Timeless Allure

First Printed Edition: 2010
First Hardcover Edition: 2016

McClure, Marcia Lynn, 1965—
The Rogue Knight: a novella/by Marcia Lynn McClure.

ISBN: 978-0-9827826-5-1

Library of Congress Control Number: 2010941668

To Grace,

For the magnificent smile you own!
Thank you for giving me, my heart, my memory…
such a beautiful thing to draw upon!
AND
For you on…your birthday!
Happy birthday, Beautiful G.C.A.E.

CHAPTER ONE

The snow was falling harder now, the wind pushing it into drifts against the buildings lining the cobblestone streets. Knight knew if he did not find shelter soon, the harsh elements would mark the end of him. He was a powerful man, but even he could not withstand such extreme exposure to such brutal weather—and winter was thickening like cold, miserable gravy. At least they'd left him his breeches. All the worse it would have been if he'd been left in nothing but his undergarments, or simply his bare skin. Licking the blood from the corner of his mouth, he shook his head, thankful for his breeches, at least.

Strapping his strong arms across his exposed chest in a feeble attempt to warm himself, Knight stumbled through the alley toward the light at the back of one of the finer houses in the square. He suspected this lighted access was the servant's entrance of the manor and hoped a kind-hearted kitchen maid or butler would allow him to warm himself by their fire until he could decide what to do next.

His knuckles were sore and bleeding—worked raw with defending himself during the earlier altercation—the fight that had left him battered and only half clothed in the dead of winter. Still, he raised one tenderized fist and rapped on the door.

❧

"The stew was delicious, as usual, Marta," Fontaine said. Brushing aside the kitchen curtains, Fontaine Pratina peered out through the window into the dark of winter's night. The dainty patterns of soft frost trimming the windowpanes brought no beauty to the season for the young woman. Winter was settling in early, and the knowledge caused Fontaine to involuntarily shiver, even for the comfortable warmth of the cozy kitchen. Winters were dark and cold and ever so long—at least, so it seemed. Especially since her parents had both succumbed to fever two winters previous, leaving the guardianship of their only daughter to her mother's sister, Lady Carileena Wetherton.

"Thank ya, Miss Fontaine," Marta said, smiling. "I added a wee bit more basil to tonight's stew. I think it was a fine decision."

Fontaine smiled at the plump, elderly woman—delighted with the cook's obvious pride in her culinary skills.

"Still, it would be wisdom for ya to run away from the kitchen before yar aunt finds ya dallyin' with the cook and scullery maids again, Miss Fontaine," Marta reminded.

Fontaine sighed. "I know, Marta," she said. "But this is the only place I feel happy anymore."

Raising a chubby hand to the girl's cheek, Marta smiled. *The poor, dear child,* she thought. She loved Fontaine as if she were her own flesh and blood. It was torturous to watch her suffer so. The girl was lovely—within and without. An average-sized young woman with thick golden hair and deep brown eyes embellished with long, dark lashes, Fontaine had the heart of an angel. Never had Marta known a person of aristocratic lineage to bear more true compassion and kindness toward her fellow man. As sweet as pudding and as fair as a princess, Fontaine treated the servants at Pratina Manor as her equals—sometimes as her superiors. And it had reaped a great deal of grief upon the young woman at the hand of her sharp-tongued, wicked aunt. Marta secreted the hope of a wonderful, dashing young man arriving astride his magnificent white stallion one day and whisking her sweet Fontaine off to a life of love and happiness.

Yet she knew the kind of woman Lady Wetherton was, her wicked intentions, her greed. Lady Wetherton had married at the age of sixteen Lord Wendell Wetherton, who had squandered away his fortune to gambling debts, leaving Lady Wetherton a nearly destitute widow at the age of twenty-six. Fontaine's parents, Lord and Lady Pratina, had taken her in and dearly paid for her vices and follies. Still, they'd named her as their only daughter's sole guardian, and Marta feared the worst kind of life for her sweet Fontaine.

"Still," Marta continued, "she'll be wicked angry if she finds ya here again, my sweet," she told the girl.

"I know," Fontaine sighed.

The kitchen was quiet now—supper long over and everything tidied and put away for the day. The soft crackle of the fire in the hearth and Marta's lulling humming of an old Irish tune lent to the comfort of the evening. But a moment later, a sudden pounding on the kitchen door startled everyone. Fontaine's own heart leapt in her bosom almost painfully for the surprise of the noise.

"For mercy's sake!" Marta exclaimed. "Who could be out at this hour…in such bitter weather?"

Being closest to the entry and desperate to stop the mad pounding, Fontaine opened the servant's entrance door leading to the alley. What met her eyes instantly sent the hairs on the back of her neck to prickling.

"Shut him out, miss! Quickly!" Daniel, the head gardener, shouted as everyone in the room stood, mouths gaping open in astonishment at what stood in the doorway.

"Please, miss," the stranger's hoarse voice begged, "just a moment of warmth is all I ask."

Filling the doorway was an enormous measure of a man, completely bare save a pair of tattered breeches—his mouth bleeding, one eye blackened and swollen nearly shut. His skin was red with exposure to the cold, and the flesh at the knuckles of his fisted, trembling hands was ragged and bleeding.

"I am no villain, miss," he breathed, "though I was set upon by several and find myself in need of shelter."

"Shut him out, miss! Hurry!" Daniel ordered again. But Fontaine paused, mesmerized by the stranger's condition and the deep green of his eyes.

"I promise you, miss…" he muttered. "You've nothing to fear from me. I…I…"

In the next moment, Fontaine found herself struggling to support the man's weight as unconsciousness enveloped him, felling him forward against her.

"Help me, Daniel! Quickly!" she called over her shoulder. The man's weight was far too much for Fontaine to support, and she felt her knees buckling under the strain of it as she wrapped her arms around him and struggled to hold him up.

Sally, one of the kitchen maids, hurried over to assist Daniel and Marta as they helped Fontaine to ease the large man down onto the floor. He made no move, no motion to indicate that consciousness would be his again anytime soon.

"He's been robbed, he has," Marta whispered.

"He's a mountain if he's a molehill," Sally added.

"He's none but trouble, Miss Fontaine," Daniel warned. "None but trouble."

Fontaine drew in a deep breath. "He's a man in desperate need, and I mean that we should help him." The dark-haired man would typically be quite powerful, Fontaine noted as she studied the sculpted muscles of his torso and arms. "Whoever would be ignorant enough to beset such a man as this?" she wondered aloud.

Daniel shook his head. "This ain't no wounded kitten, miss," Daniel said. "From the looks of his hands—"

"From the looks of his hands, he gave them that harmed him a good accountin' of himself," Marta interrupted.

Looking around quickly, Fontaine said, "Help me get him into the sickroom, Daniel. We can't let Aunt Carileena find him."

"That be for sure and for certain bein' that she's between lovers…uh…suitors at the moment," Marta said. "This one would find himself in her venomous web before he could say Jack's Jenny!"

Fontaine felt the lump in her throat creep down into her stomach. "I was thinking more that she might throw him back out to suffer in the elements, Marta." But in truth, her thoughts had been the same as Marta's. Her aunt was the most unscrupulous woman she'd ever known, and she knew that a man such as this would catch her eye quick as a wink. And for some reason, Fontaine did not want her aunt's eye catching sight of this stranger.

"He weighs more than a horse!" Daniel complained as he, Marta, and Sally helped Fontaine drag the man into the nearby room used to nurse ailing servants back to health. The room was small and dark, and Fontaine knew her aunt generally took no notice of sick servants. The man would be well hidden there.

"And just how would you be knowin' what a horse weighs, Daniel?" Marta grumbled. Daniel glared playfully at Marta, and she winked back at him.

Once they had managed to drag the stranger into the small sickroom adjoining the kitchen, Fontaine set about in caring for him. "Daniel…you'll need to strip him of his breeches and put some dry ones on him before I can tend to anything else."

"If you insist on baiting the sleeping lion, miss," he grumbled as he turned to leave. "I'll have to get something of Big William's. He's the only one who's got something to fit that in there."

"Warm water, washcloths, and towels, Marta? Please?" Fontaine begged. Then turning to Sally, she pointed an index finger. "Now, Sally," Fontaine began, "this is one of those instances in life when silence is of the essence. Not even your own mother can know about this. Do you understand? It would go very badly for this man, myself, and anyone else who helped me were my aunt to find out." In fact, Sally was two years older than Fontaine, but in the past, Sally had shown an innocence of knowledge where Lady Wetherton's character was concerned. Still, the look on her face at that moment encouraged Fontaine. Sally feared Lady Wetherton as much as any of the rest of them, it was clear.

"Yes, miss," Sally agreed. "I'll not speak of it to a living soul."

Fontaine smile and sighed with relief. "Good. Now…build a fire in here quickly, and then run along and let me know if anyone is coming toward the kitchen. Yes?" Sally nodded. In a few minutes a warm fire burned in the sickroom hearth, and Sally had posted herself in the hallway to watch for anyone who might unexpectedly arrive.

Kneeling beside the bed where the stranger lay, Fontaine took one of his battered hands in her own and softly said, "As soon as

Daniel has found you some warm breeches, we'll have you bathed and see what can be done about the damage inflicted upon you."

As she reached across the man's massive chest to pull a blanket over him, the stranger's free hand caught her arm in a tight grip.

"Where am I?" his deep and quiet voice asked.

His grasp had startled her, but realizing he was incapable of rendering immediate harm, Fontaine released a relieved breath. Putting her hand on his forehead to soothe him, she whispered, "You're safe...at Pratina Manor. But I must ask you to remain very quiet...for your own welfare. Very well?"

Suddenly the stranger's hand released Fontaine's arm and took hold of her chin, pulling her head toward his. "Have I placed you in danger?" he whispered.

Fontaine was hypnotized for a moment by the flash of his eyes— like candle flame reflected in emeralds. "No," she lied in a whisper. "No, of course not."

The stranger seemed to relax then, for his hand slipped from her face, and he closed his eyes once more.

Fontaine found her breath short and uneven. Never had a man dared to touch her so roughly, so improperly, and she was surprised by it. She was even further surprised by the odd thrill that fanned out in her bosom when he'd held her face in his callused hand. Her aunt must never find this stranger. Never!

Fontaine rose to her feet, wringing her hands, disturbed over her immediate possessiveness for the man on the bed before her. She needed distraction from her unsettling feelings and was thankful when Marta returned carrying two bowls of water and with several linens draped over one arm.

"Thank you, Marta," Fontaine said, smiling, so relieved to have someone else in the room with her.

"He's a bit on the tattered side, that's for certain, it is," Marta said, shaking her head with compassion.

"How long do you think before he'll be well enough to leave?" Fontaine asked as she set the bowls of water on the floor beside the bed and knelt down, soaking a cloth in the warm water of one.

"Days...in the least of it," Marta answered. "You'll have to be on yar toes, miss...or yar aunt will have ya for supper."

"I know it," Fontaine whispered.

"Remember how furious she got when ya brung home that wee pup last spring?" Marta continued. "Imagine how angry she'd be over this big dog."

"I know, Marta, I know," Fontaine reminded the woman. "But what was I to do? Leave him to die in the street?"

"Maybe he's a criminal that's just this evenin' escaped from prison to come and murder us in our beds," Marta offered.

"Maybe he's a prince who was set upon by thieves, and he'll reward us all when he's himself again," Fontaine countered.

Marta giggled. "That's ya for certain, miss...always the silver linin'."

"Mark my words, Miss Fontaine," Daniel whispered as he entered the room carrying a pair of men's breeches. "No good can come from taking in the likes of that one."

"And behold," Marta said, irritatedly rolling her eyes, "the black prince of gloom."

"Now, Daniel," Fontaine began, "haven't you read of the Good Samaritan?"

Daniel nodded. "I have. But he wasn't looking at a man the size of an oak, now was he?"

Fontaine smiled. She adored Daniel. Even with his somewhat pessimistic perceptions, he was a good man and a superior gardener.

"Even so, Daniel…please, change his breeches for me so I may be about bathing him. We'll be seeing what we can do to put this oak upright. Very well?" Fontaine said, smiling.

"Yes, Miss Fontaine," Daniel relented. "But my mother always said, 'Let sleeping dogs lie.'"

"And my mother always said, 'Charity never faileth,'" Fontaine added.

If he hadn't felt so near to death's door, Knight might have chuckled at the mumbled complaints of the small man rummaging around with the bedding.

"'Tain't right for a man to be so big," the little man grumbled. "The young miss has stepped in over her head this time," he rambled on. "If the lady finds out…it's the chopping block for all our heads…including yours, you big horse."

Knight heard a deep chuckle escape his throat, though he thought his body too weak to produce it.

"Oh, so you're laughing at me now, are you?" the small man grumbled, finally stripping off Knight's breeches. "Well, one more noise out of you and I'll leave you as bare as the day you were born." Knight stifled the next chuckle, catching it in his throat a moment before it would've meant his further humiliation.

"You didn't hurt him, did you, Daniel?" Fontaine inquired when Daniel exited the sickroom scowling and muttering under his breath.

"The oaf laughed at me!" Daniel told her. "Laughed! And me…trying to be the Good Samaritan."

"And ya are too, Daniel," Marta said, smiling and patting him on the shoulder.

Fontaine reached out and took Daniel's hand for a moment. "Thank you, Daniel," she told him. "You know I need you—in so many ways—and you do so very much for me. If it were in my power, I'd..."

Instantly Daniel softened. "I know, miss," he said, smiling at the young beauty. "And you know I'd do anything for you...even if I do complain about it."

Fontaine smiled. "I know, Daniel. And I'm ever grateful and in your debt."

"Off to bed with ya now, Daniel," Marta ordered. "I'll keep the wee miss company."

With a smile and a nod, Daniel left them. "Well, let's see what's been done to the poor lad," Marta sighed, taking Fontaine's hand and leading her back into the sickroom.

Fontaine knelt by the bed again, wrung the water out of the cloth, and began softly bathing the stranger's right arm.

"What do you think befell him, Marta?" Fontaine asked in a whisper.

"Thieves. Thieves is me best guess, miss," Marta answered. "There be not one thing left about him...so I say thieves it was."

Fontaine noticed then a ring on the man's smallest right-hand finger. "Save for this," she whispered, studying the ring for a moment. It was caked with blood, and she could make no sense of its pattern in the dim light.

"His hands were too swollen from the fightin', no doubt, for the thieves to get that off, to be sure," Marta explained.

"To be sure," Fontaine repeated, gently wiping the blood from the stranger's fingers. Carefully she bathed his arms and then his chest and stomach. With each cleansing motion, she removed blood and dirt from his skin only to find severe bruising of the flesh beneath.

"It may be his ribs are broken up," Marta whispered when Fontaine pointed out a particularly severe bruise at his right side.

"Can you tell by feeling them?" Fontaine asked.

"I can," Marta assured her. Fontaine watched, her own ribs aching with sympathy as Marta's plump fingers pressed here and there on the stranger's stomach and sides. "Nothin' feels loose," Marta concluded. "Firm as stone as far as I can make out."

"Good," Fontaine breathed, relieved. "Still, do you think we should try to search out a physician for him?"

"Yar aunt would know it before he did, she would," Marta said. "But me sister, over at Fairshade…she knows an ocean of medicine. I'll be havin' her in tomorrow early. She'll do a better job of guessing at his condition than I."

Fontaine felt a worried frown pucker her brow; the anxiety rising within her was cold and uncomfortable. Still, she had hope. The man was obviously strong, no doubt resilient too. She would keep her faith and tend him as best she could.

Having tended to the man's cold, ragged feet, bathing them, and finally wrapping them in warmed linens, Fontaine rinsed a fresh cloth in the bowl of water not already red with the man's blood and began to tenderly bathe his face. She winced as she wiped the drying blood from his lips and cheeks and was astonished to find that, save for a cut at his lip and the one swollen eye, his face was completely unmarred and uncommonly handsome.

"My, my, my," Marta whispered, impressed. "Like rinsin' the dirt from a diamond, it is." And she was correct. Fontaine was astonished, struck silent at the sight of him. The stranger was undeniably the most attractive man Fontaine had ever encountered!

11

He had a squarely set jaw, strong cheekbones, a slight cleft in his chin. She remembered, and she knew she'd never forget, the bright emerald of his eyes. She imagined that conscious, healed, and smiling, this man could have his choice of women, wealthy or otherwise.

"And he's clean-shaven, he is," Marta added. "This man's no vagabond, miss."

Fontaine raised a trembling hand to brush a stray strand of hair from her cheek. The entire situation was unnerving, in the least of it—this handsome stranger appearing at the servant's entrance of Pratina Manor in such desperate need? Fontaine knew she was in danger of being severely reprimanded by her aunt if she were to find out about him. And the stranger? Fontaine clutched her throat for a moment, unable to swallow the hard lump of dread filling it. If Carileena Wetherton were to find such a man harboring within reach of her wicked talons… Fontaine feared by taking him in, she'd put the stranger in a greater danger than he'd been in before he'd stepped from the brutal night of winter to find haven in the sickroom of Pratina Manor.

CHAPTER TWO

For three long days and nights Fontaine tended to Pratina Manor's secret visitor, bathing his face, keeping him warm, administering sips of warm broth when he was conscious enough to allow it, and all the time hiding his presence from her aunt. Grateful for Daniel's, Marta's, and Sally's help, she worried for them all the same. If her aunt were to find the man in the sickroom, if she were to gain a knowledge of Fontaine's beloved friends assisting her, they would be sent away forever. Fontaine knew she could not hide the man forever and therefore hoped he would soon find his strength, strength enough to be on his way. Still, the thought of his leaving disheartened her, as Fontaine's possessive nature toward the stranger continued to grow. But with each passing hour, she worried one of the manor servants would take ill and stumble into the sickroom to discover its occupant and notify her aunt. And Lady Wetherton could not discover him! Fontaine's stomach seemed to wind itself into knots whenever she thought of her Aunt Carileena setting eyes on the stranger. Her aunt would covet the attentions of such a man, no matter his social status. She would woo and corrupt him, eventually growing tired of him and casting him off like an old stocking. Lady Wetherton knew nothing of caring and compassion. She knew only

13

exploitation, and more than anything, Fontaine did not want to see the handsome stranger secreted in the sickroom fall prey to her wicked ways. Thus were Fontaine's musings as she tended the stranger on the fourth day following his arrival at Pratina.

His whiskers were longer, thicker now from days of growth, and Fontaine wondered if she should attempt to soothe him by bathing his face. She pressed the warm, wet cloth against his forehead, hoping it gave him some unconscious respite. She noted the swelling around his eye was gone, leaving a bruise, and even that had lightened a bit.

She pressed the cloth to his cheek, startled as his strong hand unexpectedly took hold of her wrist. As narrow as the stranger's gaze was through his barely opened eyes, their emerald tint flashed brilliant in the low light of the room.

When he did not speak, Fontaine calmly stammered, "You…you are harboring at Pratina Manor…my home. My name is Fontaine Pratina, and I caution you to remain quiet. You are yet in a great deal of discomfort, no doubt."

"The others," the man began, but a dry cough halted his words.

Fontaine retrieved a glass of water from its place nearby and drew it to his lips, allowing him to drink from it. "Do not speak. You are weary, and—" she began.

"The others…you've harbored me in danger to yourself," he said. "I've heard the others speak of it."

Fontaine understood he must've heard Marta and Daniel talking at some point when they were tending to him. "I have no fear for myself," she told him. "However, it would go better for you if…if we keep your presence here secret."

The stranger scowled and tried to sit up, but a deep grimace on his face told Fontaine he was still in a great deal of pain.

"You mustn't strain yourself. You've been badly beaten," she said, pushing at his shoulders and trying to ease him back down onto the bed. Still, she saw his jaw clench as he continued to rise to a sitting position.

"I'm stiff from being still so long," he mumbled, stretching his arms at his sides for a moment. "It's activity I need."

Fontaine frowned, concerned for him. "In moderation, perhaps."

The stranger rubbed his eyes with one large hand, studying his bruised and battered knuckles. Then, looking to Fontaine, a slight smile spread across his handsome features.

Fontaine felt her face warm under his gaze as he said, "Please tell me it hasn't been you, the lady of the manor, tending to my chamber pot these past nights."

Fontaine found her hands wringing nervously in her lap as she looked away from him and said, "The lady of the manor does not know of your presence here. I'm the 'miss' of the manor, so to speak."

His smile broadened, and Fontaine could not help but smile in return. "Still, it's not right that such a fine young miss should labor so well over a brute such as this," he said, gesturing to his wounded hands and ribs. Then he added, "I'm Knight, and I am forever in your debt, Miss Fontaine Pratina."

"You owe me nothing, save the task of resting in order that you may be completely well," Fontaine told him. She heard his stomach groan a long, aching moan of hunger. He winced and put a hand to his belly.

"Might a stranger, who has already caused you great inconvenience, beg a bite of bread or meat from his lovely benefactress?" he asked.

Fontaine smiled, delighted and relieved to see he had an appetite for something other than broth. "Of course! Of course, sir. I'll be but a moment," she told him. Standing, she put an index finger to her lips, indicating he should not speak.

Knight watched as the lovely young woman carefully opened the door of the room where he'd been convalescing. He admired her courage for, from the quiet conversation of the older man and woman who often tended him in this girl's absence, he'd gathered enough to know the lady of the manor would not approve of the young miss harboring a vagabond. Glancing back at him, the young miss smiled and then closed the door quietly behind her as she left, leaving Knight to consider his predicament.

Knight sighed and looked around the tiny room, his haven from the elements. He judged it to be the servant's sickroom, for it was bare save the bed, the fire, a tiny chair, and a small washbasin and stand. There were no windows, and the quilts covering him were well-worn and tattered. Still, he felt oddly comfortable and secure in the small room and in the care of those who had been tending him.

He thought again on the bits of conversation he'd overheard from the others. Certainly he was not himself, but he was fairly sure he had discerned the relationship between the fair Miss Fontaine and the Lady Wetherton as that of niece and aunt. He'd further surmised the aunt was not of the same character as the niece, being arrogant and lacking compassion.

His mind lingered on the young miss. She was uniquely kind, her touch soft and fragrant. And she was divine to look upon as well. What brute would deny the opportunity to be nursed by such a sweet girl? Still, he must find his health quickly, for he did not wish to cause her any harm or unhappiness. Slowly he rose from the bed, trying to ignore the tremendous aching of his body. He must recover hastily, but the stiffness of his arms and legs, the pain still throbbing at his sides—he must be patient yet.

Fontaine gasped, startled when she returned and closed the door to the sickroom behind her to find the stranger out of bed and standing near the fire.

"You must be careful, sir," she told him. "You are not yet yourself, I am sure."

Knight turned and smiled at her, and again Fontaine felt her face warm with the heat of a blush.

"Perhaps not, but I am somewhat revitalized," he told her.

"I've brought you bread and beef stew," Fontaine said, holding the plate heaped with hot food toward him. "I hope it will suffice."

"More than suffice it will, my lady," Knight said, gratefully taking the plate from her and going to sit on the edge of the bed.

Fontaine smiled, pleased to have made him happy. "I'll leave you to your meal then, sir," she said, turning to leave.

"I would beg you to stay, miss," Knight said. "Speak to me, if you will. Tell me of this place and its people. How is it that you came to let me in the kitchen, being that you are not in servitude?"

Fontaine smiled, delighted at the invitation, and sat in the chair next to the bed. "I find my comfort in the kitchen of the manor," she answered plainly. "My parents left this life two winters ago, and I am now in the guardianship of the Lady Carileena Wetherton, my aunt."

"For the fact you do not look, in figure, to find your comfort in the food in the kitchen of the manor...I would venture a guess it is the people of the kitchen you enjoy," Knight said, a mischievous smile donning his face.

Astonished, yet somehow oddly pleased the man would make reference to her physical form, Fontaine said, "Yes. Indeed, it is the company of my friends in the kitchen I take pleasure in." Carefully then she asked, "And…and where do you find comfort, sir?"

The man flashed a knowing smile at her and paused to take another bite of warm stew before answering. "I find comfort in travel and hard work, miss," he said. "As of late, I have worked as a stableman, a coachman, a woodsman, and a gardener."

Fontaine felt somehow saddened by his answer—not by the fact he was a hard laborer but that he found travel as his way of life. An unsettled man was this. Still, she ventured, "How came you by us?"

Knight nodded and set the plate on the bed at his side for a moment. "I walked to this town from Westchester and found no trouble 'til I passed the Dalley."

"The drinking establishment in the Fobble district?" Fontaine asked.

"I believe so," Knight confirmed. "It was already dusk. Suddenly, by way of an alley, five men pounced upon me to rob me." He raised one arm and looked at the now purple and green bruising at his side. Fontaine glanced away for a moment, disconcerted by the sudden awareness of his bare, well-sculpted torso. Although she'd seen him thus before, his conscious state unnerved her now.

"I am good in a battle, one to one…even three to one. But I fear the odds were too great for me, and I failed," he explained, studying the scabs on his knuckles. "Fortunately, I managed to keep my breeches about me…though the ones I find myself in now are not mine."

Fontaine began to shake her head when he looked at her and raised a suspicious eyebrow.

"Oh, no, no, no! It was Daniel changed you from the old ones to these. Not I," she assured him. "And I've just this morning sent Marta out for a new set of clothes for you."

"I thank you, miss...but dread to tell you I've no means of repayment," he said, "being that I was robbed and—"

"You needn't worry on it, sir," she said. "I ask nothing from you in return."

"I can work, as payment for your care, the food I've eaten, the clothing—" he began.

"That isn't necessary, I assure you," she said, feeling rather miserable suddenly. "We'll see you healthy and on your way."

Knight noticed the cloud of misery that passed over the girl's expression. He was certain she wanted him to stay, but she seemed simultaneously determined to have him leave as quickly as possible. He was intrigued. What was amiss in this grand house that would find its young miss floating between her aristocratic position and the lower classes?

And so he ventured, "Surely you have something, some task that needs doing that would serve as repayment for all you've done for me. Allow me to satisfy my pride at least and—"

"Quickly, miss!" came a voice from the other side of the door. "It's the Lady! Just at my heels, she is!"

"Sally!" Fontaine called, going to the door. "Slow her, if you can, Sally! Please!"

Knight frowned. The girl was positively terrified.

"Quickly, Knight!" she told him in a whisper, tugging on his arm to get him to stand. Sliding the plate of food under his bed, she took his hand and moved toward the door. In the dim light, he hadn't noticed the small closet behind the door, but when Fontaine opened the closet door and began rather shoving him inside, he understood at once. She was hiding him.

"Not a sound," she whispered as she began to shut him in the tiny closet.

"Nor from you," he whispered, taking hold of her waist and pulling her in with him, shutting the door a moment before the other opened.

Fontaine held her breath, tried to remain calm as Knight's arms closed around her like steel bands. It would've been dreadful enough for her aunt to find her nursing this stranger, but to find her locked away in a closet, enfolded in his arms!

"Who has been ill?" she heard her aunt ask as she stepped into the room.

"'Tis I've been under the weather a bit, milady," Marta answered. "Just restin' a bit more this mornin' between meals, I was."

Fontaine closed her eyes tightly, waiting for her aunt's venomous retort. But when none came, she felt hope rise in her bosom. Her aunt liked Marta, if indeed her aunt were capable of truly liking anyone.

"Very well. But there's no need to waste wood on a fire in here once you're feeling better," Lady Wetherton said.

"Yes, ma'am," Marta agreed.

"And let's hope dinner is served on time. We've guests arriving, you remember, Marta," Lady Wetherton added.

Fontaine heard the door to the sickroom close, but as she moved to leave the confines of the closet, Knight's arms stayed her.

"Shhh," he whispered in her ear. "There is always wisdom in an extra moment to be certain."

Fontaine squeezed her eyes tightly shut. This man was dangerous! His effect on her was wildly unsettling. His mere touch tantalized her senses beyond anything she'd ever experienced before; his breath on her neck sent gooseflesh prickling the length of her body. She must see him healed and out of her aunt's reach as soon as possible—though she doubted he would ever leave her own mind.

"There now," he whispered. "'Tis safe enough now." His arms left her, and Fontaine felt oddly cold and insecure as he pushed the closet door open, allowing her to step out. Taking his hand, Fontaine tugged at him, urging him to take to the bed once more.

"I must be found elsewhere in the house," she explained. "She only comes to the kitchen when she's seeking me out." Panic was rising in her bosom, and Fontaine knew her aunt must find her promptly, or suspicion would begin to grow in her mind. If Lady Wetherton's curiosity at her niece's activities were kindled, Fontaine would find herself under constant scrutiny and unable to return to Knight. And that thought—she could not bear it.

Knight rested his head on the bed pillow at last, and Fontaine drew a quilt over him. He caught her hand and pressed a grateful kiss to the back of it.

"Thank you, miss," he whispered. "I would surely have died had you not taken pity on me."

Fontaine drew her hand away from him, the flesh where he'd kissed it burning with delight.

"When you are well and safely on your way…only then may you consider yourself to have found good fortune," she told him before she scurried away.

Knight frowned. What was amiss at Pratina Manor? Never had he seen a more nervous and frightened young woman of means. And to do good in secret? Most aristocracy flaunted their "charitable works" as an ornament, an embellishment to buoy their pride. But to hide such as she had done for him? It was more than merely odd, and Knight meant to discover the reasons for it. Oh, he would heal—but perhaps a bit more slowly than was necessary, all the while careful to protect his young benefactress. Yes, no harm could come to her through him.

"Where have you been, Fontaine?" Lady Wetherton snapped upon finding her niece hidden away in a library window seat.

"I've been but here, Aunt," Fontaine lied. It was a lie, and she knew it, and it was one of the things she resented most about her aunt's character—the fact she must lie to her in order to do good.

"What dawdling…reading in the library," Lady Wetherton spat.

Carileena Wetherton was small, but only in stature, and her black hair and pinched nose gave her the appearance of some witch scarcely disguising herself with a sum of beauty. As a child, Fontaine had imagined her Aunt Carileena was indeed that—a witch masquerading as a woman of elegance and means.

"Reading enlightens the mind, Aunt," Fontaine told her.

One of Lady Wetherton's thin eyebrows arched indignantly. "Slothfulness softens it," she countered. "Now," she began then, "as you know, we've important guests to dinner tonight."

Fontaine sighed. Her aunt's important guests were always rather elderly men of great wealth whom she coddled in order to win suitors. Fontaine never understood why her aunt insisted she attend such gatherings. It was her aunt who was looking for luxury and wealth in the form of a husband, one who would soon die and leave her to spend his hard-earned prosperity in peace. Fontaine longed for the next ten months to hurry by, for then she would be nineteen, and as per the stipulations in her parents' will, she would inherit and be free of her aunt's guardianship. But for now, with another one of her aunt's ridiculous dinner parties, ten months seemed an eternity.

"Lord Sloan will be attending tonight and Lord Prudice, Lord Greenville as well," Lady Wetherton said, her eyes flashing with excitement. "His wealth is immeasurable, as you know."

"No one's wealth is immeasurable, Aunt," Fontaine mumbled.

Instantly Lady Wetherton's expression pinched into an annoyed frown. "You're counting the months 'til you leave my care, I know," she rather growled. "But be reminded, Fontaine…your welfare is my responsibility at present." The woman inhaled deeply, searching for calm again. Smoothing her dress, she forced a smile and continued. "And as part of that responsibility…it is needs be I teach you proper etiquette. That is why I have these social gatherings, dear—that you may master the proprieties of being mistress of your home." Again Lady Wetherton sighed. "I care not for them, save it be for your benefit."

Fontaine bit her tongue. Oh, how she wanted to lash out, to scream, to tell her aunt she was no dim-witted child! Fontaine knew full well her aunt's intentions toward such gatherings; in ten months' time when Fontaine inherited, Lady Wetherton would be left penniless if she didn't secure herself a new husband. Once in a while, she pretended to care about Fontaine's welfare, but Fontaine knew it was only pretense—only an attempt to make Fontaine feel obligated somehow in the event she needed to live her parasitical life by feasting on Fontaine's inheritance. And so, there was nothing Fontaine could do, save to play the match until she was free to win it.

"I know, Aunt," Fontaine sighed.

Lady Wetherton smiled rather triumphantly. "Good girl, darling," she said. "Now, I want you to wear that green frock we picked out last week, and don't be late." She took Fontaine's hand. "I'll relieve you from the frivolities of the conversations before dinner…but I want you at the table promptly. Understand?"

There would be no tending to Pratina's secret stranger until much later, and Fontaine was loath to the idea of dinner with the lords and her aunt. Still, she forced a smile and nodded.

"Yes, Aunt," she relented. "As prompt as a pussycat on a pillow."

Lady Wetherton sighed with irritation. "Too much time in the company of the servants, Fontaine. Ladies of title and wealth do not compare themselves to pussycats and pillows."

"Yes, milady," Fontaine agreed. Oh, how she wanted to scream and slap the woman.

"And then," Sally continued, "then it comes to light through her own father's will that Lady Wetherton is to be her guardian! And that the young miss can't inherit her money or her freedom 'til she be nineteen years of age!"

"That is an odd age to set," Knight mumbled. He liked this Sally. She'd come into his room more than an hour before to check on him, at Miss Fontaine's request. When she'd found him awake, she promptly sat down at his side and began spilling information without stopping for breath. Knight, although not one to take advantage of people in most instances, began baiting her with questions. His benefactress had taken a great risk in helping him, and he felt greatly indebted. Perhaps he would learn something through this kind kitchen maid that might help him repay Miss Fontaine Pratina somehow.

"What of marriage? What if she were to marry before she reached nineteen?" Knight asked. Perhaps there was hope for the girl, a beau on her arm ready to carry her away from her aunt's tyranny.

Sally's eyes widened, and lowering her voice she said, "Before the age of nineteen, Miss Fontaine cannot marry without Lady Wetherton's permission. And it even goes so far as to say Lady Wetherton can choose someone to marry the young miss to…whether Miss Fontaine wishes to or not. So states the will. And believe me," she said, nodding for affirmation, "Lady Wetherton won't permit her to marry no one…unless he's of Lady Wetherton's choosing." She moved closer to Knight, and he listened carefully as Sally again dropped her voice. "And that's why Marta says Milady is having these dinners. She's auctioning the good miss off to the highest bidder. That's what Marta says."

Knight frowned. It all sounded too dubious to believe. But if he knew nothing else, he knew of the wit and insight of the servants of a house. Their knowledge and assumptions, though sometimes marked with flaws, were more often than not exactly right.

Knight found serenity elusive once Sally had left him to himself once again. He could hear the scuffling about in the kitchen beyond, the preparations for the dinner, and he was angry. He saw no way of helping the poor girl, for if he were found out, it would go very badly for her. Still, he would think on it—think on her, the poor girl.

"And was it a lovely dinner party, miss?" Marta asked as Fontaine entered the kitchen dressed in her lovely new green frock and wearing the expression of the bitterly miserable.

"I think she's chosen Lord Greenville as her next victim," Fontaine said. "He's the most wealthy of the three, after all."

Marta smiled and threw her arms around Fontaine's shoulder. Fontaine returned her embrace, drawing the warmth of loving friendship into her soul. Marta's hugs always uplifted her, and she was able to smile.

"Put it from yar thoughts now, me lass," Marta cooed. "Put it from yar thoughts."

Fontaine released a deep sigh as she turned toward the sickroom. "And how goes our little patient?"

Marta smiled, "Well enough. He's on the mend, he is."

"That's good," Fontaine said.

Marta knew Fontaine was restraining herself from going into the stranger's room. She'd seen the way her eyes lit up whenever she thought of tending to him.

And so she said, "None of us have looked in on him in some time, we haven't, miss. Might be wisdom to do it now." Marta smiled when Fontaine's eyes began to twinkle once more. Still, she wished the stranger in the other room had turned out to be some dashing man of power and means who could spirit her sweet friend away instead of a coachman wandering the world.

Fontaine stood, studying Knight's face as he slept. He appeared serene, as if he were truly resting. His brow had often been puckered when he'd slept previously, an expression, a grimace of enduring pain, while unconscious. But now, now he seemed quiet and so much healed. Fontaine bit her lip, scolding herself silently for wishing for a moment he'd heal more slowly. For three days he'd given her blessed escape from the reality of her circumstances—distraction in the form of needing her help, and with his uncommonly handsome countenance. What would she do when he had gone?

Carefully she pulled at the quilt covering his legs, drawing it up over his torso.

"A peaceful slumber I wish you, Knight," she whispered.

When she'd closed the door behind her, Knight opened his eyes and sighed heavily. Tucking his hands behind his head, he stared at the ceiling of the small room for a long time. Surely something could be done to help the girl, but helping her in the obvious manner would be too revealing, too dangerous. Neither could he linger long, lest he be found out. Therefore, how to help the unfortunate girl eluded him.

He lay awake for a long time, until the scuffling in the kitchen had ceased, until the house was quiet and still—until the sun broke over the rooftops and the scuffling in the kitchen began anew.

CHAPTER THREE

The day Fontaine Pratina had been dreading had arrived. It was with heavy heart she watched as Knight put on the new coat Marta had found for him. Even though she was overjoyed that, after seven days of convalescing in Pratina Manor's sickroom, Knight's strength seemed fully returned, she had dreaded his leaving. And now, here he stood, handsome and healed and preparing to leave her.

"Them breeches fit fine, they do," Marta said, prideful in her ability to judge Knight's size so perfectly. "The boots too. And the coat."

Knight smiled at the cheerful woman. "You've certainly a gift for dressing a man," he said, chuckling at Marta's resulting blush.

Attempting to appear indifferent and calm, Fontaine stepped forward and stuffed several notes into Knight's coat pocket.

He immediately withdrew the tender and held it out to her. "No, miss. I'll make my way in a day or two," he told her.

But Fontaine forced a smile to mask her aching heart. Shaking her head, she said, "Please accept the sum, Knight. I'll not sleep a wink thinking of you penniless while enduring another winter's night."

Clenching his jaw, he sighed heavily. Fontaine knew his pride was hurt by her offering of the sum. Still, better his pride than his hide, she thought. She felt her hand go to her throat, attempting to stifle the emotion rising there as she watched him fasten the buttons on the heavy coat Marta had purchased for him.

"If you ever need help…" Fontaine began, but his eyes locking on her own, their emerald fire flashing with determination, silenced her.

"If *you* ever need help, miss," he told her. "Write to me at the March Inn in Pemmbrook. I know the innkeeper, and he'll be able to contact me."

For a brief moment, Fontaine felt her heart leap with the possibility of seeing him again. Yet she knew it could not be, for were her aunt ever to set eyes on Knight, he would certainly be lost to her.

At the very thought of her Aunt Carileena, panic began to engulf Fontaine, and she urged Knight, "Thank you, Knight. But I would see you safely on your way now, before—"

"Who have we here, Fontaine?" Fontaine's hand tightened around her own throat at the sound of her aunt's voice behind her. "And what are you doing in the kitchen…again?" Lady Wetherton said, stepping up to stand beside her niece.

Knight had seen this kind of woman before—a wealthy, manipulative aristocrat with nothing better to do than spend her husband's money and flirt with servant boys. His distaste for the kind of woman that now stood studying him from brow to boot was complete. Further, he noted the way the color left Fontaine's lovely face, the way fear crept over Marta's expression. So this was Fontaine's venomous aunt.

"A…a man seekin' a position at the manor, he is, milady," Marta said. She was quick on her feet, and Knight could see Fontaine was ever grateful for it. "I saw Miss Fontaine passin' and asked her to speak with him."

"I've…I've explained we've no need of extra help at this time, Aunt," Fontaine stammered.

Knight's eyes narrowed with curiosity. It was all the more clear to Knight then. The young miss of the manor did not want him to stay, and he could guess why. She cared for him. She did not want to see him fall prey to the wiles of her aunt.

Then to Knight, Fontaine began, "Again I'm sorry I cannot offer you a position at Pratina Manor, sir. But we have—"

"One moment, Fontaine," Lady Wetherton interrupted, placing a hand on Fontaine's shoulder to stall her. Knight watched the frown of painful defeat pucker Fontaine's brow, watched something akin to anguish cloud her lovely brown eyes.

Lady Wetherton stepped closer to Knight, and he forced an accepting smile. "What skills do you have, young man? What posts have you held previously?" she asked.

Knight glanced at Fontaine as she stepped back, conceding defeat in her aunt's wake. And he knew then—a game was afoot, and he was not one to back down from a challenge.

"Of recent I was coachman to Lord Tarria of Pemmbrook, milady," he answered. "But I'm suited to any post requiring hard labor as well."

Fontaine felt her stomach churn with disgust as her aunt mumbled, "I'm certain you are." Even Marta's reassuring arm about her shoulders did nothing to comfort Fontaine. She'd lost. Again she'd lost to her aunt, and this loss was the most painful she had ever known.

She gazed up rather longingly at Knight. What a beautiful man he was, if men could be called beautiful. Not simply in appearance, but he'd treated her with respect and gratitude. In the confines of the tiny sickroom he'd talked with her, been genuinely interested in her existence. Not to mention the thrill he'd given her the day he'd pulled her into the sickroom closet with him, securing her tightly in his strong arms, causing her to feel safe, if only for a few blessed moments. But now he would be lost to the wiles and cunning ways of her aunt.

"Coachman?" Lady Wetherton repeated. "Why…why, that's perfect! I've been without a proper coachman for years," the witch exclaimed.

Fontaine looked to Marta, who shook her head in disbelief. Lady Wetherton had a perfectly wonderful coachman in Big William. Furthermore, Big William had been driving the Pratina family coaches since before Fontaine was born. Surely her aunt did not intend to put such a loyal man out simply because Knight had caught her fancy? Fontaine knew she did intend it, however, and she could not simply stand silent.

"What…what a wonderful notion, Aunt," she ventured. "Big William can serve as my own from now on. I'm old enough for my own coachman, am I not?"

Lady Wetherton inhaled deeply as she studied her niece. Finally, she said, "Yes, Fontaine, dearest. I believe that you are. Goodness knows it's time for you to learn how to better distinguish between your place and the place of those who serve us." Fontaine swallowed her anger, for Big William's sake. "And William is old enough to know his place," Lady Wetherton added, somewhat glaring at Marta for a moment.

Returning her attention to Knight, she said, "It is settled then. You shall be my new coachman, Mr....Mr...."

"Knight, milady," Knight offered. "My name is Knight."

"Knight, is it?" Lady Wetherton repeated. "My coachman, Knight. I like that," she said. "Well then, welcome to Pratina Manor, Knight. I hope you don't mind travel, for we only hail here for the winter. Spring, summer, and most of autumn we spend in the country at The Graces in Shetlands. The Graces is our country manor, and we actually prefer it to town," Lady Wetherton explained.

"I prefer the country as well, milady," Knight assured her.

Fontaine felt as if the contents of her stomach might very well empty at her aunt's feet, and she knew she must escape. "I suppose, since you've nicely arranged things, Aunt...that I may be about my business," she said.

Lady Wetherton breathed a laugh, a scoffing sigh. "What business could you possibly have to be about, my dear?" she asked. "Still," she continued, her eyes appraising Knight once more, "why don't you toddle along and inform William of his lovely new position as your coachman? I'll show Knight the carriage house and the rest of Pratina."

"Yes, Aunt," Fontaine mumbled.

Knight was angry—infuriated at the way the woman belittled the kind girl, his rescuer. Yet an idea had shaped in his mind, and he must be patient, calm, and agreeable if he were to eventually succeed in helping the young miss.

Still, when Fontaine's tear-filled eyes met with his one last time, he wondered if he could indeed endure the elder woman in the hope of somehow helping the younger.

The tour of Pratina Manor, the explanation of his duties in the company of Lady Wetherton, was almost more than Knight could stomach. With each new door opened, the lady found cause to stumble, forcing him to catch her arm. Her conniving smile as she studied him from brow to boot, again and again, caused him to want to take her throat in hand and, in the very least, growl at her. For two hours she occupied his company, and by the time she had handed him over to Minerva, the housekeeper, in order that she might show him to his quarters, he thought his patience would be unable to endure her one moment longer.

Once in his quarters, however—quarters he was to share with Big William, the true and worthy coachman—he exhaled a deep and calming breath. He had not possessions on hand to organize, simply the clothes on his back and the money in his pocket, both provided by the kind Miss Fontaine. He must seek her out—let her know, somehow, he hadn't betrayed her. He knew she frequented the kitchen in the late hours of evening. He would find her there then, he was certain, and he would express the truth of where his loyalties were placed. He would make her believe it, for he owed her more than could ever be regained.

"She's a villain, that one," Marta grumbled, "and she taints anythin' she touches, she does."

Fontaine sat at the servant's table in the kitchen, her chin resting in the palm of one hand. She stared at the candle flame in the center

34

of the table, listening to Marta and trying to find some joy in her friend's chatter.

"Still," Marta continued, "I hope Knight is different, I do. I like to think that he is. He seems stronger than most men she corrupts…wise to her ways."

"He's a man, Marta," Fontaine sighed. "And like any other man, he's drawn to wealth and beauty…no doubt driven by vanity and physical desire."

"You think no better of me than that?" Knight said, entering the kitchen at that moment.

Fontaine felt the sting of shame's blush tint her cheeks as he strode toward the table, taking a seat beside Marta and across from Fontaine.

"And to think I've sought you out to assure you I'm not ignorant, only to find you judging me so quickly." His voice was deep and angry, and Fontaine could not meet his gaze for shame's sake.

"If ya're different than other men she's known, than ya've yet to prove it," Marta mumbled, "for ya've fallen into her aunt's clutches easily enough, ya have, Knight."

Fontaine stared at her hands, wringing anxiously in her lap, but she gasped when she felt Knight reach across the small table, taking her chin in hand and raising her face toward his.

"I've not betrayed you, miss," he said, his hand on her face causing her breath to quicken, her bosom to flutter.

"Ya're a brazen one, ya are!" Marta exclaimed. "To touch her the likes that ya have!"

But Knight ignored Marta, and Fontaine could not help but be captured by the smoldering heat of his gaze.

"I owe you my life, miss," he told her. "And I mean to repay the debt as best as it can be repaid. You saved me, after all," he said.

"God saved you, Knight," Fontaine corrected, afraid to trust him any further. After all, he belonged to her aunt now.

"With you as His instrument," he countered. "And I do mean to prove to you…that I mean only to serve you."

"I *have* a coachman," Fontaine said, her voice breaking with emotion, tears barely withheld in her eyes.

Knight inhaled deeply, dropped his hand from her chin, stood, and walked around to Fontaine's side of the table, kneeling beside her. Taking her hand in his, he pressed the sum of tender she'd gifted him earlier in the day and fisted her fingers around it.

"I mean to serve you, Miss Fontaine. I've a debt to repay, and I will repay it," he told her. "With or without your faith and trust in me."

Fontaine felt her breathing stop as she tried not to feel belief in his promise. In truth, she wanted nothing more than to throw herself into his arms and beg him to leave her aunt's service, for she knew she could not endure watching him fail in his promise. But worse, she could not endure the thought of her aunt in Knight's embrace the way she had been in the sickroom closet. And Fontaine knew it was Lady Wetherton's intention—to be bound in Knight's arms, to be lost in his affections. Fontaine grimaced at the vision of her aunt's being the recipient of Knight's attentions, his embrace—his kiss.

"You've no idea…the strength of her will," Fontaine whispered.

"You've no idea the strength of mine," he said in a lowered voice.

The emerald of his eyes burned through the brown of Fontaine's until she felt she might lose all hold on reality and fling herself against him, begging for him to choose her instead of her wealthy and powerful aunt. Her thoughts of wanting to own him were foreign, unexpected, and she found great difficulty in banishing or absorbing them. He was a stranger to her! She knew nothing of this man—nothing more than the fact he was divinely handsome, lethally attractive, strong, and seemingly chivalrous. How could she possibly want to own him or be owned by him? Putting a hand to her temple, Fontaine struggled to dispel the mixture of emotions swirling about in her being. She must not succumb! He wasn't to be trusted—not with the way he apparently fell so easily into her aunt's sticky web of cunning deceit.

"Off with ya now, Knight," Marta ordered. "She's too much concerned over the state of things this night, she is." Coming to stand by Knight, Marta took his arms and urged him to his feet. "Off with ya, lad."

"You can put your trust in me, miss," Knight said as Marta led him from the kitchen. "And your faith."

But as soon as his back was turned, a torrent of tears and quiet sobbing wracked Fontaine's body with heartache and pain the like she'd never imagined. Oh, how she wanted to trust him, to feel safe in his presence at Pratina. But she knew what Lady Wetherton was capable of, and Knight, strong though he may be, had most likely never encountered the likes of her. Her aunt would woo him, win him, and take him for her lover. And when she grew weary of him, she would send him off on other travels.

Then a more miserable thought entered Fontaine's mind. What if her aunt never grew tired of Knight? What if he turned out to be the one man who truly won her cold, cruel heart? Burying her face in her hands, Fontaine sobbed, vented the tears and heartache of the bitterly unhappy.

"Don't ya be professin' any great loyalty to the lass, 'less you mean to show it, my lad," Marta warned as she rather pushed Knight out of the kitchen and into the hallway.

"You know I'm beholden to her, Marta," Knight growled, angry the woman didn't believe his sincerity.

"I know ya are, I do," Marta sighed. "But…but the situation for Miss Fontaine is bleak, I fear…and no manner of false hope will help her endure it any better."

"I don't intend that it is false hope," Knight said. He couldn't fully understand why everyone distrusted him so, simply because he'd accepted Lady Wetherton's offer of employment at the manor. Surely they didn't think a salary would turn him. And surely they didn't imagine her wicked feminine wiles would ensnare him. Still, as he looked at the plump, rather adorable woman's expression of concern, he realized they knew nothing much of him in fact—just that he had been set upon by miscreants, had been beaten nearly to death, and felt grateful for their help.

Marta sighed and forced a compassionate smile. "How old are ya, lad?" she asked.

Knight chuckled. "Old enough to read the hearts of women," he answered.

Marta's smile broadened. "Oh, I've no doubt ya're old enough to fool with the hearts of women…but to read them?" She shook her head and added, "I judge ya're not a day over twenty-four, and it takes a man of fifty years in the least…to read the hearts of women."

Knight smiled and nodded, amused at the woman's insight and humor. However, her next utterance purely astonished him.

"Just promise me this, me lad," she said, dropping her voice to a whisper and tugging on his sleeve in order that he would bend his ear closer. "Ya'll kiss our young miss once…before you surrender to the witch's ways."

Knight felt his eyes widen, more astonished at the cook's suggestion he kiss Fontaine than the inference he would eventually succumb to Lady Wetherton's wiles. "What say you, Marta?" he asked.

"Ya well heard what I said, ya did," Marta told him. "Furthermore, ya'll kiss our young miss *first*…before ya take the kiss of the devil's bride."

Knight could only stare at Marta, unbelieving.

"Now, off with ya at last, lad," Marta said, turning from him. "I've the kitchen to tend, I do."

In truth, Knight had already considered on what the taste of Fontaine's lips would be, for he looked on her as any man would—as a young and beautiful feminine treat who had rescued him from certain tragedy. Still, as Knight lay in his bed that night, the rhythmic sound of Big William's snore doing nothing to lull him to sleep, he thought on Marta's astonishing suggestion again and was somewhat irritated.

"They've no faith in me whatsoever," he whispered to himself. *Still*, he thought then, *having been given permission—nay, having been ordered—to kiss the fair miss of the manor…then who am I to disobey?*

And so Knight resolved—when the opportunity presented itself, he would take the pleasure of Fontaine's soft and no doubt innocent mouth with his own and feel no guilt in it.

Fontaine wiped the tears from her cheeks and turned her pillow to its other side, its current surface having become far too damp with her sobbing to remain comfortable.

"Why do I concern so?" she asked herself out loud. "He's a traveler, a rake, no doubt. Certainly he feels an obligation toward me," she mused. "But that is the stuff of it…an obligation."

Yet why can't I put him from my thoughts? she wondered in silence. *Why can't I stop the terrible fluttering in my bosom that begins at the mere sight of him?*

Being a young woman of aristocratic birth and fine social standing, Fontaine was not unaccustomed to the attentions of men both young and old, both homely and handsome. Thus, even for his uncommonly attractive presence, it was beyond her understanding as to why Knight had rapt her soul so completely.

For a moment she thought, *Have I fallen in love with him?* But she knew one did not fall in love with a stranger over the course of seven slight days. Yet she felt her body yearning to be close to him, envisioned the green blaze of his eyes each time she closed her own, longed to hear the deep nature of his voice, wished for the sound of his low chuckle in her ears.

Finally, amidst the soothing crackle of the fire and the memory of those beloved moments in the sickroom closet spent wrapped in Knight's arms, Fontaine found sleep. However troubled it may have been, Fontaine found respite in the unconscious dreams of Knight.

CHAPTER FOUR

"I've such compassion, such understanding, for my sweet niece and her circumstances," Lady Wetherton explained.

"I see it daily, Milady Wetherton," Knight said, gritting his teeth.

In the three weeks since gaining employment at Pratina, he'd also gained further insight into the plight of his young rescuer, Fontaine. Through the servants' gossip, Marta's and Big William's friendships, and most of all by way of his own observations, he'd learned the full depth, the deep hopelessness, of Fontaine's situation.

Fontaine's parents had failed miserably in trying to provide proper care for their only daughter. Most likely assuming they would never pass away together, their will not only named Lady Carileena Wetherton as their daughter's guardian until she reached the age of nineteen; it also stipulated that Lady Wetherton must choose, or at the very least approve of, any suitor interested in their daughter until such time as she reached the same age. Further, Lady Wetherton could condone or deny Fontaine's marriage to any suitor or even pledge her troth to a worthy man of Lady Wetherton's choosing once her niece reached the age of eighteen, the age deemed appropriate for marriage by Fontaine's parents. Supplementary to the already contemptible terms of Fontaine's marriage or troth, if she did marry before the age of nineteen, her entire inheritance, including properties and all tender, fell to her husband, thereby becoming solely his own set of assets.

Thus, Knight understood why Fontaine's outlook was so bleak, her hopes so suppressed. And short of throwing her into a sack, tossing her over his shoulder, and spiriting her away, he was at a loss as to how to help her. Still, he had decided to bide his time, wait patiently, and see what other opportunities might present themselves.

Enduring Lady Wetherton, however, had proved a greater challenge than he had surmised. She was undoubtedly the most flirtatious and forward woman of title he had ever encountered. Her access to the Pratina wealth had spoiled her as well. She was a woman used to getting what she wanted—anything she wanted. In truth, Knight gained a decidedly deeper understanding of Marta's concern where he was concerned, for it was apparent Lady Wetherton found him attractive. He saw nothing in her, however, save the countenance of malevolence. Still, for Fontaine's sake he was enduring Lady Wetherton's orders, attentions, and wicked ways.

Lady Wetherton placed her hand on Knight's arm and smiled up at him. "I knew I could trust you to show loyalty toward me the moment I saw you, Knight," she said.

Knight's jaw clenched so tightly the grinding of his teeth echoed in his head. She meant to seduce him. He knew it, and he was sickened by it—further sickened because he was not certain how to avoid Lady Wetherton's advances and remain in her employ, thereby protecting his young miss.

"Yes, milady," he said through clenched teeth.

Lady Wetherton tossed her head, a wicked smile spreading across her face. "I see that Fontaine has taken a fancy to you, Knight," she began.

Knight's brow puckered, for he was surprised and puzzled by the venue she chose to cast her lure. Lady Wetherton laughed, amused by his expression of puzzlement.

"Oh, Knight! Silly man. Do not feign ignorance in the matter," she said. "You can't have missed the way her eyes brighten when you enter the room, the way a blush rises to her cheeks when you smile at her."

"Apparently I have, milady," he said. So this was it! She planned to further abuse Fontaine by jealousy's means. His molars ached with sealing the anger in his throat threatening to vent at the woman.

Again the lady smiled at him. "Your humility becomes you further, Knight," she said. "However," she continued, "I've a proposition for you. Let us see if you're game, shall we?"

"Milady?" Knight asked, truly puzzled.

Lady Wetherton sighed, affecting disquiet. "You see, Knight, Fontaine's prospects in life…well, as you may have noticed, she isn't the loveliest of young ladies." Again Knight's molars ground into one another with irritation. "Furthermore, the responsibility of finding her a suitable, worthy husband…unhappily falls to me. And though I've several superior prospects, it is a sad thing to see a young woman enter into a marriage of convenience with an older, albeit capable man some twenty years her senior, without ever having known the affections of a young, handsome, mischievous man such as yourself."

Knight's eyes narrowed. The woman's loathsome character seemed boundless. Was she indeed suggesting…

"Therefore—and I assure you, you will be well paid for it—therefore, I propose a gift, as it were, to my dear, neglected Fontaine," Lady Wetherton said, smiling at him.

"That being?" Knight prodded. He could not believe she was actually suggesting what his imagination interpreted.

Lady Wetherton laughed again and said, "A harmless tête-à-tête…a secret lover all her own, and in you, my dear coachman!"

"I beg your pardon, milady?" Knight mumbled.

"She'll fall in love with you, naturally. But…it needs be, for I know how desperately a young girl's heart needs a secret love to comfort her as the years pass. And I do so want that for Fontaine," the woman explained. "As for your benefit, not only am I giving full permission for you to romance my niece…but your reward shall be the equivalent sum of two years' employment here." Lady Wetherton smiled, her eyes flashing with triumph.

Knight knew full well what the woman's intentions were: heartache, pain, and injury to Fontaine. To place in her memory and heart a lover after whom she'd pine away for the rest of her life, simply assuring her complete unhappiness in the arranged marriage she must face. Still, his mind was racing with the possibilities the situation might afford. For one, it would procure time in his favor—time to consider other ways of rescuing the rescuer from her sad ruin.

"Two years' wages, milady?" Knight asked.

Instantly Lady Wetherton's witch's eyes blazed with triumph. "Two years' worth, Knight."

He pretended to be pensive for a moment. "What rules bind me?" he asked plainly.

"Your wisdom shows in that question," she said. Still smiling, she said, "Only a few. It cannot be an advertised affair…to the servants or any other. It must remain in secret, for her reputation must be protected at all cost."

"Of course," Knight mumbled.

"She must think it is in earnest, as well," the woman continued. "Fontaine must believe that you are indeed smitten with her."

Knight nodded.

"And finally…" Knight noted the smile fading from her face, indicating the seriousness of her next utterance. "Finally…it ends when I say it ends. No questions, no arguments…and you move on," she said, reaching up, caressing Knight's cheek with the back of her hand. "You move on to…other venues of entertainment."

The sickened condition of Knight's stomach, the anger swelling in his chest, and the need to lash out verbally at the witch almost overcame his desire to help Fontaine. But with every ounce of power coursing through his being, he restrained his want to overcome her.

"Are those the only restraints put upon me?" he asked through still clenched teeth, for her hand on his cheek infuriated him.

Lady Wetherton sighed with delight at her seeming victory. "Yes," she said. "Other than, as I said, her virtue must remain untainted…at least, to the world's knowledge."

"Then, milady…the game is afoot," he finished.

"Marvelous!" Lady Wetherton chimed, clapping her hands together. "It is so important that a woman have her cherished memories, Knight. I hope you can understand that."

Knight forced a smile and nodded. "Oh, I understand, milady. I understand entirely."

"The crone knows no end in her corruptions," Big William said.

Fontaine paused before entering the kitchen, for she'd heard Knight's voice in conversation with Marta and Big William and could not help eavesdropping.

Big William had been able to spend more and more time in the company of Marta and the other servants who frequented the kitchen rooms. Since being reassigned to the position of Fontaine's personal coachman, Big William had been able to enjoy many more hours of much-deserved rest and simple time, and Fontaine was happy to see it. Big William, an elderly man in his sixties, unusually tall, and now white-headed, had served the Pratina family for nearly thirty years. Fontaine trusted and loved him and was glad to see him so less overworked and with time to sit for a change. Furthermore, he'd become fast friends with Knight, who showed the man nothing but respect and comradeship. Knight's kindness to Big William only served to further fluster Fontaine, for with each passing day, Knight seemed to seep deeper and deeper into the meat of her heart. In fact, of late, she'd taken to avoiding him, certain he could read the delight in her eyes whenever they met. But something about this conversation interested her above others, and so she waited, listening.

"She'll be rushin' to hell in a bushel basket when the time comes, she will," Marta said, lowering her voice.

"Still…it would keep the young miss safe…for a time, perhaps," Big William added.

"Then…then you think I should play at being her lover?" Knight asked.

Fontaine's hand flew to her mouth to stop the scream of heartache begging release. It had come already? In only three weeks, her aunt meant to abandon Lord Greenville for Knight? Further, were Big William and Marta in agreement with the travesty? Choking back her tears, she thought, *At least he only means to play at it…instead of being heartfelt in his intended attentions toward her.* But the thought did little to soothe her pain, and she wanted to know no more of it.

Entering the kitchen, Fontaine said, "And what are you three gossiping about this evening, then?" All three glanced away guiltily for a moment. "May I join you?"

"In fact," Knight began, "I would speak to you a moment privately, if you would allow it, miss."

Fontaine was somewhat touched, for it appeared as if he meant to confess to her as well as he had to her friends. Did he then consider her to be one he could confide in? It was a comfort, but a harsh one.

"Very...very well, Knight," she stammered, her heart beginning the strike in her bosom like a mad hammer.

Knight rose from his seat at the kitchen table and motioned she should enter the sickroom with him. The wild beating of her heart was deafening in her own ears as she entered the sickroom, Knight closing and bolting the door behind them.

"I'm not certain this is entirely proper, Knight," she began. Her nerves were getting the better of her. His proximity in the tiny room, which held so much meaning for Fontaine because of their moments together during his convalescing, caused that she should begin to tremble slightly.

"Begging your pardon, Miss Fontaine," he said, lowering his voice and smiling at her, "but the two of us have spent a great deal of time alone in here on winter's nights not too recently passed."

"What...what did you wish to speak to me about?" she asked, for she could think of no further argument to offer. And she feared she would faint from heartache if she lingered on those beloved memories any longer.

She watched as a frown puckered his brow and he drew in a deep breath as if preparing to present the worst kind of news. Instantly, Fontaine felt a sort of feral panic begin to rise in her. Did he mean to leave Pratina? Was he leaving her so that he would avoid her aunt?

"First, I must beg your confidence, silence of this matter, and...and complete trust, miss," Knight said.

"You…you have it, of course," she managed, though she thought she might melt at his feet in tears of beseeching him to stay, to abandon her aunt and become her own.

"Very well," Knight began. Fontaine was momentarily distracted by the brilliant flash of his eyes, by the pure magnificence of his face and form. But his next words drew her back to reality.

"Your aunt approached me today with…with the suggestion of…of an arrangement."

"That being?" Fontaine said, her voice breaking and betraying her withheld emotion.

Knight seemed anxious, and Fontaine understood why. To tell her of her aunt's intentions toward him must indeed be difficult. Yet part of her began to loathe him for it.

"For the sum equivalent to two years' wages…" he stammered.

Fontaine closed her eyes for a moment, sickened by the realism her aunt truly offered to pay Knight for his attentions.

"For two years' wages, she has asked that I…that I…" he stammered.

Fontaine was pleased he felt it hard to utter the fact to her at least. "Pay court to her, so to speak?" Fontaine finished for him. She turned from him as a tear escaped her eye, traveling down one cheek.

"To…to pay court to *you*, so to speak, miss," he finished.

"What?" Fontaine exclaimed, whirling about to face him, indifferent to the fact tears were now streaming down both her cheeks. "What did you say?"

Knight swallowed hard, cast his eyes to the floor, and answered, "She wants me to persuade you…win over your affections."

"Wh-wh-why?" Fontaine sobbed. It was a cruel trick! The cruelest her aunt had ever conjured. And Fontaine knew instantly that her aunt had been able to read her emotions better than she thought. She felt she'd hidden her feelings for Knight deep enough that no one could find them. But she hadn't.

"Please don't cry so, Miss Fontaine," Knight begged, an expression of enduring agony passing over his face. "I…I think…I think it isn't all bad. She…she wants you to have…to have a…a relationship…a pleasant relationship to remember after…"

"After I'm married to some elderly, crippled lord who will care for me until he dies and I am left a young widow? Is that what she told you?" Fontaine shrieked.

"Please, miss. Lower your voice. She'll hear you and—" Knight rather commanded.

"She means me no pleasant memories, Knight!" Fontaine sobbed. "She means to harm me, break my heart, and…"

In the next instant, Fontaine found herself wrapped tightly in Knight's supremacy. He'd reached out and clamped a strong hand over her mouth, pulling her back against his chest and strapping her there with his free arm.

Tears fairly flowing from her eyes, she felt her breath leave her as he put his mouth to her ear and whispered, "You must keep quiet, miss…lest she hear you and discovers my allegiance does not lie with her." Fontaine could feel the coarseness of his whiskers on the flesh of her neck, his hot breath on her cheek, and she wanted nothing more than to melt into his arms, beg him to protect her, to love her and keep her with him.

"I mean to repay the debt I owe you, Miss Fontaine Pratina," he continued in a whisper. "And if playing the secret lover to you allots me more time to consider on how to do so…then I well mean to play at it." All resemblance to a humble coachman was gone from him. From his rather rough handling of her to the resolve in words, Fontaine sensed nothing but dominant determination in him. Even in the way his lips softly caressed her ear as he spoke did she feel of his inimitable strength.

"Now," he whispered, "may I count on your being rational—and quiet—if I release you?" Fontaine nodded and squeezed more tears from her eyes. He seemed unconvinced and, removing his hand from her mouth, demanded, "Promise it."

"I…I promise it," Fontaine breathed.

"Very well," he sighed, releasing her. Yet when he did, she only longed to return to his arms, to be held securely against him, to feel his breath on her neck.

"She has ordered that I cannot speak of this to anyone," he told her. Fontaine did not turn to face him again, however, for tears were still falling to her cheeks. "But well you should know by now my loyalty is not to such as her, and I ask you…what would you bid me do?"

She turned to him then, not caring if he should see her crying. "I would bid you leave here!" she exclaimed in a whisper. "I would bid you to save yourself from her evil ways, her ability to corrupt the lives of others!"

"She's no power to corrupt me, miss," Knight assured her.

"She corrupts everything she touches! In one way or the other, everything in her wake is damaged," she sobbed.

"Even if it is true…you fight it, do you not?" he asked.

"What do you mean?" Fontaine sniffled.

"Have you followed suit of her? Integrated her ways, her mannerisms, her corruption into your own soul? No, you have not. You have remained true to what you believe to be right and wrong. Why do you then hold so little faith in me?" he asked. When she could not answer, for she did not want to reveal all she was to him, he continued, "I'll tell you why—because I am a man. It is as simple as bluebird's song. Men have betrayed you. Oh, not men like Big William, Daniel, or your father. Other men…the men she associates with. No doubt they've shown no unyielding symptoms of morality…and you count me the same."

"You do not know her the likes that I do," Fontaine whispered defeatedly. "Aristocracy…it is a corrupt breed of human being. Wealth and personal pleasure are all it holds as valuable, and I loathe being born to such a class."

"You are not like her…or those who align themselves with her," Knight said.

"Am I not?" Fontaine said, as an unusual contemplation began to fill her mind. She wanted Knight for her own—wanted his smiles to be to hers, wanted to be in his embrace. Was she really so much different from the other women of her association? "And you, as good as your intentions appear to be…you think this…this farce will somehow defend me from her will where I am concerned?"

"I think it may procure further time needed for me to repay the debt I owe you, yes," he said.

He was quite chivalrous, if rather misdirected in his belief that chivalry still triumphed. And there was the reality that she was in love with him. With all her heart, Fontaine knew in those few moments spent in the glow of Knight's intended heroics, she loved him. And perhaps her aunt was right. Perhaps she would thank her aunt one day, thank her for forcing this astounding man to pay his attentions to her so that she could look back on him as a beautiful dream she held once upon a time.

Wiping the tears from her cheeks and straightening her bodice, Fontaine said, "Very well, lover. Would you enlighten me…inform me of the rules of engagement in this matter?"

Knight smiled at her. "You trust me then?"

"I trust that your intentions are valiant, Knight…and who knows what is to come? Perhaps the earth will take to quaking and swallow Aunt Wetherton up before she has a chance to damage anyone further," she answered.

Knight chuckled and drew a handkerchief from his breast pocket. "Perhaps it will, miss," he said, offering the cloth to her.

Fontaine accepted the handkerchief and dabbed at her eyes. "The rules, then. For I've no doubt she had stipulations."

"She did indeed," Knight admitted. "First, our affair must be in secret. No one is to know of it," he explained. "Of course, I've already told Marta and William…and you."

"Of course," Fontaine said, smiling. This detail in itself gave her comfort; that he cared for her above her aunt, in this it was obvious.

"Second, you must believe me to be in earnest," he said. "Therefore, miss…you must act as if you've some secret happiness tucked away."

"Of course," Fontaine said again. And she thought then this part of the farce might come easily enough, for she would have a secret happiness tucked away—a knowledge she had gotten the better of her aunt for once.

"Third…" Knight paused. "Third…it ends when she commands that it ends."

"Thus, we are assured we have an unmeasured amount of time for you to whisk me away from my pitiful existence as an heiress of aristocracy," she said.

"Yes," he unwillingly admitted.

"And what of you then, dearest Knight?" Fontaine asked. "Are you then to receive compensation for…another farce such as this?"

"You know her better than I think, it is clear," he admitted. "But I promise you this, miss. When the task is done and I have repaid my debt to you…somehow…I will quit this place before she has a chance to offer me another amusement."

Fontaine let her eyes plead with him and reached out, taking hold of his arm as she said, "I ask that you leave when the task is done…whether or not you feel you have repaid the obligation you feel toward me."

"If I fail, I'll not abandon you to—" he began.

"Promise me, Knight," Fontaine pleaded. "Promise me you'll leave when it is done…no matter the outcome on my behalf." She could not see him fall further prey to her aunt's conniving. Selfishly, she would have his attentions for her own for a time—allow him to believe he could help her. But then, then he must be put away from the evil that now permeated her own life.

He appeared as if he might argue the point with her for a moment, but the pleading in her eyes must have influenced him. "Very well, miss. If I fail to help the earth open up and swallow your aunt, or otherwise to liberate you from her clutches…I will take me leave of this place, as you wish," he said.

Fontaine sighed, relieved. In his promise to her, she knew Knight would be safe. Eventually.

CHAPTER FIVE

"Still," Fontaine began, encouraged by the mischievous twinkle in Marta's eyes as she told her friend of her agreement with Knight, "I find...I find I am greatly unsettled about the entire affair."

"Affair?" Marta giggled.

Fontaine smiled and shook her head. "You know what I mean, Marta," she said. "How does one proceed?"

"Oh, I've no doubt in me that Knight will ensure ya know exactly how to proceed, me lass," Marta said, a delighted smile emblazoned across her face.

"It's all in pretending, Marta," Fontaine reminded her. Yet she was quite unsettled with the excitement that rose in her bosom each time she thought of perhaps receiving Knight's attention. "You've no reason to seem so amused." Fontaine considered for a moment. "Still, he seems so deeply earnest in his desire to help me—to be prepared, willing to go to such lengths on my behalf. It is very sweet of him."

Fairly slamming the wooden spoon she'd been using to stir her pudding down onto the stove, Marta said, "Sweet of him, is it? It's nothin' less than heroic!" Her eyes narrowed in an expression of concern. "Ya do realize the consequences far him were he to be found out, do ya not, lass?"

In truth, Fontaine had tried to put the possibility of her aunt learning of Knight's disloyalty out of her mind.

"She'd have him whipped, in the very least of it! Beaten and thrown out! And he'd find himself in worse condition than he was when ya let him in this very servants' door, he would."

"He cannot be found out, Marta," Fontaine told her, "no matter the consequence to me."

"There can be no consequence to either of ya," Marta said. "We must be certain of that, we must."

Fontaine tried to swallow the worry, the anxiety rising in her throat. She had agreed to play a part with Knight, but she wondered if she should've simply denied him and taken whatever bitter pill her aunt had in store for her. Since her conversation with Knight the evening before, she'd questioned whether the entire episode should have been avoided at any cost to her own well-being.

"Yet the fact remains, Marta," she began again. "What am I to do? How can I possibly convince Aunt Wetherton I am in earnest in my affection for him?"

Again Marta smiled. "With all the wisdom ya have far one so young…it amazes me yet the innocence ya have, as well, it does."

Fontaine was rather defensive about the remark. "I am not wholly naive, Marta," she reminded the woman. How could Marta imply such a thing? After all she'd seen Fontaine endure? Fontaine well knew the kind of woman her aunt was. Still, although she said nothing to Marta, she failed to see what her aunt would expect from her niece under such circumstance as having a secret lover. Her aunt knew Fontaine was morally upstanding, even if Milady Wetherton herself was not. Surely her aunt did not expect a secret lover to corrupt her in any way.

"Oh, but innocent ya are, lassie," Marta began. "If ya weren't such a sweet soul, ya'd know well enough a man such as Knight….well, he'll be havin' no trouble makin' clear and certain to yar aunt that the two of ya are…involved."

Fontaine frowned, still perplexed. What would be expected in convincing her aunt? Should she smile at Knight often in her aunt's presence? Perhaps force an occasional blush when he was in the room with her?

Fontaine sighed and shook her head. "Well, she knows how firmly I feel in matters of morality. Certainly she does not intend that I should be corrupted in any manner."

Marta laughed and then said, "Of course she intends, lass!" Taking a seat next to Fontaine at the table, she explained, "She certainly intends it. It's in her very nature it is…to make yar life as miserable as she can. Oh, she's playin' the sympathetic angel, she is…tellin' Knight she's wantin' ya to have a lovely, tender romance before marriage. We all know her far better than that, we do! What she wants is to see yar heart broken, fill ya with regret and longin'. And that, me darlin', that alone is corruption…of the soul, it is."

Marta was right. Carileena Wetherton was a wicked woman, and she knew Fontaine was not. Fontaine knew her aunt did not give up on procuring Knight herself simply out of kindheartedness and concern for her niece. No, her plans were as selfish and villainous as ever they had been.

"I should never have agreed to this, Marta," Fontaine sighed, burying her face in her hands. "It can only make matters worse and…"

Her speech ceased as Knight strode into the room, quite unexpectedly.

"Miss Fontaine," Knight said in a whisper. "Quick!"

"Pardon?" Fontaine asked, startled into rising from her chair.

"Your aunt is on her way to the kitchen," he explained. "The game is afoot!" The daring smile on his face, the brilliant fire in his eyes, gave Fontaine no comfort, and as he took her hand, she withdrew it instantly.

"Oh, don't forsake bravery now, peach," he chuckled.

"Peach?" Fontaine exclaimed, her hand still tingling from his touch.

"Away with you now, Marta," he ordered. "Let her find us this way alone."

With a smile and a nod, Marta slipped from the room by way of the servants' door to the alley.

"Make be the proficient actress, miss," Knight said, lowering his voice and taking hold of her hand once again. "You've got a splinter in this finger, just here," he whispered, separating her index finger from the rest, raising it closer to his face and scowling as if concentrating with great intention on the digit.

"I do?" Fontaine whispered.

"You do," he ordered. Fontaine was not dull-brained, just caught unsuspecting for a moment. After all, these were her first moments drawn into the ruse. "Here she comes now," he whispered. "Stay still."

From the corner of her eye, Fontaine could see her aunt pause at the kitchen doorway.

"It's just there, miss," Knight said, no longer whispering. His eyes narrowed for a moment, an alluring smile spreading across his lips as he said, "Indeed a nasty splinter you've got there, miss…but not to worry." Fontaine gasped, her eyes widening with astonishment as Knight then drew her finger to his mouth, placing the end of it on the tip of his tongue a moment before tenderly nibbling at it with his teeth. Her knees buckled, his conduct suddenly stirring her in a manner she'd never before experienced. She straightened her traitorous joints and managed not to collapse in rapture at his feet somehow. Knight's eyes remained locked with her own, and Fontaine felt the crimson of titillation's blush burning her cheeks as his nibbling the flesh of her finger slowly grew into two lingering kisses, administered in warm, moist succession.

"There you have it, miss," Knight said, releasing her hand and pretending to pluck something from his tongue with his thumb and forefinger.

"Oh!" Fontaine breathed. "Thank...thank you very much, Knight," she stammered, completely flustered by his intimate performance.

"I'm always glad to help, miss," he said, smiling.

"Here you are, Knight!" Lady Wetherton sang, entering the room. "I've need of my coachman today. I'm off to luncheon at Lord Greenville's estate."

"Yes, milady," Knight said with a nod. "I'll ready your carriage at once." Nodding in Fontaine's direction, he said, "Miss?"

"Yes. Thank you, Knight," Fontaine managed.

Wearing a mischievous grin, he left the kitchen.

"And here I find you in the kitchen once again, Fontaine," Lady Wetherton sighed. "How many times have we spoken of this?"

"I...I had a splinter, Aunt...and...and was seeking Marta's help," Fontaine explained. "She seems to be out, however."

Lady Wetherton smiled as if she owned some secret triumph. "And your splinter?"

"It…it is no more," Fontaine answered. "Actually, Knight was able to retrieve it nicely."

Lady Wetherton breathed a laugh. "I'm certain he was." Then, taking her gloves from her reticule, she added, "Well, I'm off to luncheon with Lord Greenville. Pray occupy yourself with your needlework or in the library and leave the servants to the kitchen, Fontaine."

"Yes, Aunt," Fontaine said.

Once Lady Wetherton had left the kitchen, Fontaine exhaled with relief. She realized from the moment Knight had entered the kitchen, her manner of drawing breath had been rather shallow. Taking hold of the kitchen table, she promptly sat down and attempted to settle her nerves.

"What a display indeed!" Marta exclaimed in a hushed voice as she stepped through the servants' entrance door, radiating delight. Clapping her hands together with excitement, she added, "That will put her to thinkin' all is as she's ordered, it will." Sighing understandingly then, she covered one of Fontaine's trembling hands with one of her own soft, plump ones. "And ya were thinkin' it would be hard to seem as if ya were enjoyin' his affections. Why, ya're red as a rosy radish, lass!"

"His manner was far too…too flirtatious, Marta. Far too flirtatious!" Fontaine said, trying to still the mad hammering in her bosom.

"His manner was perfect, it was! Just what the old hag wanted," Marta assured her. "He did a fine job of it. Quick on his feet, he is." Marta tenderly took Fontaine's chin in hand, smiling. "But ya'll need to learn to be far quicker on yars, me girl."

"I know it," Fontaine admitted. "Still, I doubt this façade entirely, Marta. No good can possibly come of such deceit."

Marta laughed. "Oh, ya're not doubtin' it entirely, me love…else ya wouldn't have agreed to it in the first place."

Fontaine closed her eyes, gently massaging one temple. "He gave me such hope last evening, Marta. For a few brief moments, I began to believe he might actually deliver me somehow."

"And he might yet do it, me love," Marta whispered, smiling lovingly at the girl. "He might yet do it."

Knight was glad of the fact the winter rain was not pouring down upon him that afternoon as he sat with Lady Wetherton's carriage outside Lord Greenville's manor. Winter was waning; he could sense spring around the corner, and he was glad for it. He sat down on a nearby bench, pulled one of Marta's nutmeg muffins from his pocket, and ate it entirely in only four bites.

A smile captured his lips as he reflected on the expression arresting Fontaine's face when he'd put her finger to his mouth during those moments in the kitchen earlier. For an instant he feared she might faint away from the shock of it, but with a flutter of her lovely eyelashes, she had managed to recover quickly. The situation was lacking insight on his part, for he should've guessed she was wholly untouched by any such flirtation. Still he chuckled at the memory of her gasp, the way her cheeks blushed vermilion.

"Poor little kitten," he muttered aloud to himself. She definitely needed schooling in the art of making love and in the skill of deceiving. His smile left him, for he was reminded just what a master of deceit he had become during his stay at Pratina Manor. Drawing in a deep breath, he tightened his jaw, however, reminding himself it was the only way to help her—the only way she would accept, in any case. He would not reveal himself now and lose all her trust he'd worked so hard to gain. He would see the charade through, every bend in it, until the poor girl was in better circumstance. Still, guilt gathered thick in his throat as he thought of her innocence where his true character was concerned. He sighed and stood when he saw Lady Wetherton descending the steps of Lord Greenville's manor house.

One thing he knew—he must not let Fontaine be caught so unaware again. He must tutor her before next her aunt found them together. At first, Fontaine's astonishment at his attentions would be anticipated. But Lady Wetherton would expect that to change, expect her niece to be more at ease with him eventually.

Yes, Knight thought as he helped Lady Wetherton into her carriage. *The peach must not be found so unripe next time.*

Fontaine could not push from her mind the memory of Knight's attentions to her in the kitchen. All day she had tried, keeping as busy as she possibly could. However, each time she turned to another task, the feel of his lips on her finger burned anew, and she could think of nothing, save the fire in his eyes as he'd kissed it. And the more she contemplated the episode, the more she knew how wholly unprepared she was to employ her part in such a role.

And thus, she found herself pacing the floor of her bedchamber as night fell, struggling with exactly how she was to extract herself from the situation.

"I simply cannot continue with this," she said aloud. "She'll see through my deceit at once!" she told herself. But what of Knight? What of the two years' wages her aunt had promised as payment for wooing her niece? No doubt he was in desperate need of such a sum. And what of his desire to repay the obligation he felt he owed her?

"Oh dear! Oh dear!" Fontaine mumbled, her hands nervously fidgeting as she paced back and forth.

A soft knock on the bedchamber door startled her, and she put her hand to her bosom to calm herself. Whatever could someone be about at such an hour?

"Come in," she called but gasped, her eyes widening, as Knight himself stepped into her bedchamber, bolting the door behind him. Quickly, Fontaine snatched the white velvet robe from the foot of her bed and held it up in front of her. To have him catch her in such a state, swathed only in her nightdress, her hair down about her shoulders and arms—it was scandalous!

"Knight?" she exclaimed, taking several steps backward. "You can't be here!"

He seemed unconcerned as he looked at her for a moment, his eyes traveling the length of her and an amused grin capturing his face.

"But I'm your lover, remember?" he said.

"My pretended lover," Fontaine corrected him.

His smile broadened, and he strode toward her, saying, "Pretend or otherwise, you need instruction in the art of it all."

Fontaine straightened her posture defiantly. "What do you mean?" she said. In truth, she was rather put off by his inference she was incapable of convincingly proceeding in their farce.

"Come now, miss," he chuckled. "You nearly dropped dead at my feet this afternoon in the kitchen." He stood directly before her now, and Fontaine felt her breathing quicken at his nearness. He was too handsome for his own good! It was unnatural for a man to be so magnificent to look upon.

"You…you surprised me so entirely…bounding into the room like that with only, 'You've a splinter in this finger,' as a clue to what you intended," she defensively explained. "My aunt was quick on your heels! I had no time to prepare and—"

"My point, miss," he interrupted. "I doubt there will ever be time to prepare, and you must be on the ready next time."

Fontaine clutched her robe more tightly to her bosom. "I'm...I'm not certain there should, in fact, be a next time," she began. "I'm afraid—"

"Of course you're afraid," he interrupted again, his smile fading to a scowl. "Your future possibly hinges on the success of this deception...or the failure of it." The green blaze of his eyes was mesmerizing, and Fontaine was struck speechless for a moment.

"You must learn to accept my attentions more casually...as if you expect them...as if you enjoy them," he said, lowering his voice and moving so close to her that the front of his shirt brushed against her robe for a moment. "I want to help you, Fontaine...Miss Fontaine." He was a brazen one, she noted, to trip into using her familiar name without any formal title. Yet it delighted her somehow, caused her heart to flutter in her bosom.

He reached out, taking a long strand of her hair in hand and twisting it loosely about one finger. Instinctively she stepped back from him, shy of his attentions.

"And this, my peach...is why I've come to tutor you," he chuckled, releasing the strand of hair.

Fontaine glanced away for a moment, self-conscious of her inexperience and anxiety. "I fully admit," she began, "I've no depth of experience in the matter of taking a lover."

"And that is as it should be, miss," he confirmed. She looked back to him, somewhat encouraged. "It is exactly what your Lady Wetherton wants to change...your innocence, your purity."

He turned from her then, changing his attention and his line of subject. "You may not think it to look at me, miss," he began, "but I am an intelligent and capable man."

Fontaine was puzzled. "Have I ever given you cause to think I thought otherwise?"

He turned to look at her once more. "No. I just want to assure you of my ability to assist you. You must allow me time—time to talk to you about your situation, the terms of your father's will, the stipulations—so I may better understand how to proceed in helping you."

"My father's will?" Fontaine asked. Somehow she assumed he meant to help her by spiriting her away, softening her aunt's heart. What would her father's will have to do with anything? After all, it was ironclad. Mr. Dennis, her solicitor and executor of her father's will, had long ago assured her of that. "What do you mean?"

Knight shook his head and waved his hand in a gesture of dismissing his own remarks. "We've no time for that just now," he said. "First we must procure time—time to think, to plan, and to act. And in order to do so, miss," he said, going to stand just before her again, "in order to do so, you must play the better part of accepting me—accepting me into your life, into your arms…" He paused, lowering his voice and smiling beguilingly. "Into your bedchamber for midnight rendezvous."

Fontaine was determined to remain only as flustered as she already was. She would play the part, better than she had earlier in the day, and so she said, "You're here, in my chamber now, are you not?"

Knight smiled. "Excellent, Miss Fontaine," he said. "But you must likewise accept my affections," he added. "My touch." Again he reached out, taking a strand of her golden hair between his fingers.

Fontaine swallowed, tried to still the mad hammering of her heart, and did not pull away this time.

"Very good," he encouraged her. "Very good." He placed one hand on her right shoulder, and she flinched. "Not very good," he chuckled. Ever so slightly squeezing her shoulder, his free hand took one of her own and raised it to his face. "Be calm, miss…for you are in no danger with me," he whispered. Forcing her hand open, he raised her palm to his face, pressing it firmly against his cheek.

Fontaine had touched, actually rather caressed, Knight's face many times during the period of his recovery in the sickroom. But this was far different, and her entire being began to tremble. His skin was warm, his whiskers rough, and the sensations thrilled her.

"See there, miss," he mumbled. "You did not die for having to endure my touch."

How little he understands, Fontaine thought—for, in truth, she had nearly fainted for holding her breath and from the mad pounding of her heart.

"And now," he said, his eyes burning into her own, "a little more."

Fontaine gasped quietly as she felt his hands at her throat. Gently his hands held her, his thumbs pushing at her chin, tipping her head backward slightly, as his fingers rested at the back of her neck. Slowly, his head began to descend toward hers.

"Drop the robe, Fontaine," he mumbled, his voice low and tempting like some baker's sweet stuff. "You cannot stop my advance and retain your modesty," he taunted. "You had better make your choice swiftly."

Fontaine held her breath, for in truth, she had never wanted anything in her life the way she wanted Knight's kiss! She imagined how heavenly it must be, how completely swept from reality and into a dream she would find herself, no doubt. But courage failed her, and she let go of her robe, placing her hands to his chest and pushing at him firmly. Still, she was bitterly disappointed when he chuckled and dropped his hands from around her neck. Secretly she'd hoped he'd command the moment, kiss her even for her nervous state.

"I press you too much for one day, indeed," he said. He stepped back from her, shrugging his shoulders in a rather boyish gesture of defeat. "I feel rather cast off, actually," he sighed. "To have my attentions so emphatically refused—it's more humbling than I expected."

Suddenly Fontaine felt bad for her actions. He was indeed a man from whom any girl would desire a kiss. "Oh no, no, Knight," she began, shaking her head and stepping forward toward him. "I…I did not mean…I'm just so…"

But he chuckled and turned to leave. "Not to worry, miss," he said as he unbolted her door, making ready to leave. "Next time…I will not be put off so easily." He smiled at her, nodded, and said, "Good night then, miss." And he was gone, leaving Fontaine blushing, trembling, and yearning for his further attentions.

"This can come to no good end," she said quietly to herself. She could not deny the truth any longer, could not push it to the back of her mind, trying to ignore it as she had been doing. Marta had been right, and Fontaine knew her soul had already been corrupted, for she would never be able to push Knight from her mind or her heart now. Her aunt would succeed, had already succeeded, in hurting her.

The warning in her mind was telling her to end the farce with Knight, end it before it was too late—before he pierced her heart and soul any further, leaving a wound that would never heal. Still, with every moment in his presence, every sense of his touch, she grew weaker, the ability in her to stop the charade melting away—melting just as winter's cold cloak was giving way to spring's bright and flowery window.

At last, she settled into her bed, but sleep did not come easily, for his touch was on her skin, his face in her mind's visions. As had become habit, Knight fell all around Fontaine, and it was not until the early hours of morning that she slept.

Knight lay awake in his bed, hands tucked under his head, studying the shadows cast on the ceiling by the dying embers in the hearth and enduring Big William's continual snore. He smiled, thinking of the warm brown of Fontaine's wide and frightened eyes. Oh, he full well knew she'd wanted him to kiss her earlier in her bedchamber, for she'd noticeably paused before dropping her robe and pushing him away. No doubt she was curious, having little experience as such a young woman of her state of things did. Still, he had been a bit unsettled himself at how sincerely he'd wanted to kiss her, how the moisture in his mouth had suddenly increased as he'd first contemplated doing so. Perhaps he would have to be more careful—careful to stay ever focused on his purpose.

His purpose after all was to repay the debt he owed her and then move on to life's other experiences. He could little afford to be distracted, to let his heart become too attached to the girl—no matter how lovely she looked, her golden tresses cascaded about her shoulders, no matter how beautifully her long, dark lashes shaded her mesmerizing brown eyes. His mouth watered at the thought of her sweet red lips suddenly, and he frowned.

"The fixed mark is...to help the girl. That is all," he muttered to himself before turning over and attempting to drown out Big William's snores by crushing his pillow over his head.

CHAPTER SIX

Winter had given way to spring. Pratina Manor's lawns were dotted with robins in the early hours of morning, and hopeful hyacinth and daffodil bulbs had begun pushing young but sturdy sprouts up through the flowerbed soil. Fontaine fancied even her wicked, winter-tempered aunt was touched with a bit of spring fever, for she'd sent Daniel ahead to The Graces almost a month earlier. All residents of Pratina were to make for The Graces in a mere week, and Lady Wetherton wanted the gardens at the country estate to be well on their way—weeded, pruned, planted before she arrived.

The prospect of leaving Pratina for the freedom and fresh air of The Graces had given Fontaine new reason to delight—the prospect of The Graces and the attentions she'd been receiving from Knight over the past few weeks. Oh, he'd done nothing quite so shocking as to enter her bedroom and trick Fontaine into abandoning modesty only to leave her for want of his kiss—nothing so shocking as all that. Still, the smiles and winks he bestowed on her, the way he'd catch her arm when passing her in the hallway, letting his hand caress the length of it as she walked by, all this had caused Fontaine to find herself rather giddy.

She'd made up her mind the very morning after he'd intruded in her bedchamber; she'd made up her mind to enjoy the farce. After days of agonizing, admitting she would never be rid of his memory, Fontaine had decided to take hope in the old adage "better to have loved and lost." Her aunt had succeeded in corrupting her niece, for Fontaine knew she would never feel toward another man the way she felt toward Knight. The whole affair was too unique and wonderful to be matched. Yet Fontaine had consciously decided if her aunt was to succeed, then so she would have her memories of Knight. Heartache be hanged!

Further, with each quiet and secret conversation Fontaine had with her secret lover, she began to harbor a greater hope in his ability to help her. He was wise, not just with common sense but with academic intellect. Over and over again he questioned her knowledge of her father's will, gleaning from Fontaine every shred of possibility in interpreting it.

"Is your aunt able to visit Mr. Dennis and view the will, have it interpreted without your presence?" Knight had asked, leaning back in the bench under the big oak of Pratina's back courtyard.

"No," Fontaine told him. "I must always be present."

Knight had nodded, a triumphant smile spreading across his handsome face.

Spring was still cold, and Fontaine fought the need to shiver in the cool of morning's mist. She would not let Knight know of her discomfort, for he would no doubt lead them inside and away from privacy.

"Are you able to meet with him, view the document without her present?" he asked.

"Yes. Yes, but why?"

"Then Mr. Dennis is beholden to you, first. He is your solicitor first, your aunt's only involvement being she is your guardian," he said. Fontaine had confirmed that Mr. Dennis was loyal to her above her aunt.

"Does he merit your trust? Is he loyal to you?" Knight asked next.

"I believe so," Fontaine told him, unable to hide her chilled state any longer. Much to her surprise and delight, Knight did not suggest they return to the manor but rather slid closer to her where she sat next to him on the bench, placing one strong arm about her shoulders to warm her.

"She'll see you," Fontaine warned. Her aunt was still in her chambers, her morning habit of gazing out the window as she dressed already active, no doubt.

Knight chuckled. "You always forget, miss...that is the idea."

He sighed then, frowned, and seemed to be talking to himself more than to Fontaine as he mused aloud, "Mr. Dennis...keeper and interpreter of your father's will, loyal and sympathetic to your plight. For eight months still, your aunt can give your hand in marriage, and you will not inherit. If she marries you off, she receives a sizable sum of her own...your parents' assurance that she would take care of you. Further, if you marry before the age of nineteen, whatever brute takes you to his..."

"I beg your pardon?" Fontaine exclaimed, mortified by his inference.

Knight smiled at her and continued, "Whatever brute takes you to his...bosom...will inherit your entire fortune."

"What?" Fontaine gasped.

"It is the law of our country, Fontaine," he explained, frowning, obviously astounded by her naiveté. "Unfair perhaps, but the law all

71

the same. What is yours becomes his, peach. How could you be in ignorance of the fact?"

Fontaine sat stunned. "I…I…was only fifteen when mother and father died. I…I was so astonished by it all—Aunt Wetherton as my guardian, the stipulations of marriage—I never stopped to think about…" She put her hand to her throat for a moment, feeling as if she might be sick. "But you are right. I do know that. I've just never had cause to consider on it where my own welfare is concerned."

"This being because you are always so concerned with the welfare of others, miss," he told her.

But she didn't hear him, her thoughts already in a whirl of panic. Rising from the bench, Fontaine began to pace to and fro in front of it. "I…I've been so desperate to hide from all of it for so long, burying my head in the sand, so to speak. Oh, Knight!" she exclaimed in a frightened whisper. "If my inheritance is not my own…what will become of Marta and Big William? What of Daniel? What of The Graces? Any husband I am bound to can do whatever a whim takes him to do!"

"She'll find a titled man, no doubt a great deal older than you—one she can manipulate." Knight paused as Fontaine stared at him in revulsion. "It…it has been my suspicion all along, miss—Lord Greenville. She doesn't mean him for herself," he told her.

Fontaine's heart slipped to her stomach in a sickening lump. "Lord…Lord Greenville?" she breathed. "He is full sixty and three! And mean as a wet cat!" Fontaine began wringing her hands, panic heavy in her body. "He…he has the breath of a fortnight-fasting Father!"

Knight rose to his feet, taking her shoulders in hand. "You must remain composed, Fontaine. There is always hope," he told her.

"What hope is there?" she cried. "Lord Greenville! My stomach sickens at the thought of it! To marry me to such a man…I…I…"

Knight's eyes narrowed, his grip on her shoulders tightening as he lowered his voice and calmly said, "She cannot force you to marry…if she cannot find you."

"What?" Fontaine breathed, trying to keep hope at bay.

"You must visit your solicitor. There are some questions I must have answers to before I proceed further," he said, releasing her.

"How…how am I to visit him without her knowing?" Fontaine asked, her brain still whirling from his previous inference.

"That should be easy enough," Knight said, dropping his hands from her shoulders.

"But, Knight!" Fontaine cried, panic rising in her once more. "Lord Greenville! I should rather die than…the stench of his breath alone would drop me dead!" She scowled at her lover when he chuckled. "There is nothing whatsoever amusing about this, Knight!" she scolded.

"I am sorry, miss," he said, though still smiling. Taking one of her hands in his, he squeezed it reassuringly. "I'm certain the thought of enduring his kiss is unpalatable to you."

"Unpalatable?" she exclaimed. "Unpalatable, you say?"

Oh, she was in a temper now! Knight tried to contain the laughter rising in his throat provoked by her hysterics. He felt nothing but compassion for her plight, yet she had such a way of amusing him—even at the most serious of circumstance.

He was fascinated by the way her golden curls bobbed back and forth at the nape of her neck, the deep brown of her eyes aflame with emotion. In truth, he admired her bravery, her commitment to better the lives of the servants at Pratina. It had sincerely been her first concern; at the realization she might not gain control of her inheritance, her first thoughts were for the well-being of Marta and the others. She was a sweet, compassionate, lovely angel, and he would not let her worry any longer on the stench of Lord Greenville's breath.

"Ha!" Fontaine exclaimed, knowing full well she should attempt to compose herself. "Unpalatable? Have you ever tasted of rancid meat, Knight? Drunk the bitter curds of sour milk?"

"Settle yourself, miss." He took hold of her hand and pulled her with him. "Your aunt is about, and we don't want her thinking you find me as unpalatable as Lord Greenville."

"Where is she?" Fontaine whispered as she followed Knight toward the outbuilding, which served as both a greenhouse and protection for Daniel's gardening supplies.

"Closer than either of us would prefer," he answered. "Quickly, now…in here."

Fontaine easily followed Knight into the small building. *Like a lamb to the slaughter*, he thought to himself. A slight wave of guilt washed over him. But it vanished swiftly enough, and he closed the door behind his prey.

It was only in winter and spring Fontaine enjoyed the greenhouse, for in the summer and autumn it proved too warmly moist for comfort. Yet the scent of soil, bulbs, seed, and blooms were fragrant and pleasing to her at that moment.

"You are such a short thing," Knight mumbled as he swept aside the gardener's tools cluttering the surface of a nearby table.

Fontaine frowned at him. "I am not short," she said, smoothing her skirt proudly. "It is you who is overly tall." Then, before she had a chance to avoid his advance, assuming she had wanted to, Knight took hold of her at the waist, effortlessly lifting her up and seating her soundly on the table's top.

"What are you about, Knight?" she asked, startled at his unexpected action.

"Hush, peach. You talk too much," he mumbled as he stripped off his vest, tossing it to the floor at his feet.

"I...I do not talk too much," Fontaine stammered, unnerved by his having quit his vest. Further, he now stood before her pulling the bottom of his shirt from the hold of the waist of his breeches. "What...whatever are you about, Knight?" she asked.

"She wants me to earn my money," Knight explained. "So she told me just last evening. The time has come for me to demonstrate to her I well intend to deserve it."

"Surely you've given sufficient attention to me. I did not know she had reprimanded you." Fontaine felt ashamed at putting Knight in such a situation as to displease her aunt. She well knew the effects of causing her aunt disappointment. But why hadn't he mentioned this to her sooner?

Oh, I am a wretched liar indeed, Knight thought to himself. Still he was determined to chase any thoughts of Lord Greenville's stenching kiss from his young friend's mind. Likewise, he'd waited long enough to taste his pretty victim. His impatience was growing, and the rogue in him would be unleashed.

"Follow my lead," Knight commanded. His eyes flamed emerald, with the determination of a man to be reckoned with.

"Follow your lead?" Fontaine asked. She imagined she knew his intention but could not believe her imagination was in earnest. Her seat on the table gave her position to be staring into Knight's marvelously handsome face, as it was now even with her own. Instantly she was unable to think rationally, hardly able to breathe in being so close to him.

"She's nearly upon us," he mumbled as he struggled to untie the collar of his shirt. "Damned ridiculous clothing…" he growled a moment before stripping off his shirt and tossing it to lie with his vest.

"Knight," Fontaine gasped. "You…you go too far."

"Shhh," he whispered as his hand encircled her neck, his thumbs caressing the length of her neck from the hollow of her throat to the tip of her chin.

His emerald gaze was hypnotic, and Fontaine was lost in it as one of his hands moved to her cheek, caressing it tenderly before letting his fingers travel lightly over her lips. He meant to kiss her! She knew it, read the message in his eyes, and whether for her aunt's benefit or not, Fontaine meant to have his kiss.

Knight's left hand continued to support her neck as his other wound itself in her hair at the back of her head. Gently he tugged at her hair, causing her head to fall backward as he lightly kissed the hollow of her throat. Instinctively, lest she should lose consciousness from the euphoria of his lips on her flesh, she reached out, clutching his forearms. The warm, lingering kisses Knight began trailing over Fontaine's neck and throat caused her entire body to break into gooseflesh, and it frightened her.

As she felt her heart swelling with love for him, desire that he should continue in applying his affections, Fontaine whispered, "Knight? Knight, surely she is convinced."

"Shhh," he said again, and she felt his breath on her face as he kissed her face just at the corner of her mouth. Slowly he kissed her cheek, her forehead, the lobe of one ear, and Fontaine heard a quiet whimper escape her breath, for she knew she was lost to him.

All thoughts of her aunt, Lord Greenville, the inheritance that might never come to her—all thoughts other than those of Knight—were driven from Fontaine's mind as he left caressive kisses on her neck and face. Then letting his arms encircle her waist, he pulled her from her seat on the gardener's table and let her feet drop to the floor, pulling her body taut against his own.

Fontaine let her hands go to his chest, trying to push him away, trying to escape before she was lost to him. Nevertheless, it was too late, and the warmth of his skin beneath her palms only further weakened her already fleeing want to resist him.

Letting her hands caress the breadth of Knight's shoulders, Fontaine swallowed the excess moisture in her mouth gathering for the want of having his kiss there. She desperately wanted him to kiss her lips, but he stayed a breath away, intentionally or unintentionally teasing her somehow. She thought she might die for want of his kiss, full and thorough on her mouth, and she closed her eyes, searching for something in her mind to distract her from the want of it. But there was nothing, only the sense of his arms around her, his lips lingering at the corner of her mouth.

Charade! her mind screamed in silence. She forced her eyes open, pushing firmly against his chest.

"Enough, Knight," she breathed. "Enough."

His embrace slackened somewhat, and he looked at her, eyes narrowed as if trying to read her thoughts.

"No," he breathed a moment before his head descended, his mouth claiming Fontaine's in a deep, molten kiss, which left her senses dizzying, her arms and legs weakened to numbness.

Never had Fontaine experienced such elation, such rapture! The feel of his mouth to hers, the moist heat of it, unlocked her inhibitions, and she felt the softness of his hair feathered between her fingers, having let her hands travel from his shoulders to be lost in it.

"Mmm," Knight sighed as his kiss deepened, the sound resonating through Fontaine's head and chest like a sweet, liquid ambrosia. She would not leave him, she decided. Never! She'd stay thus occupied forever, lost in the warm, sweet taste of his kiss, the power of his arms keeping her safe.

But as Fontaine resolved to remain rapt in Knight's kiss eternally, Knight's intentions seemed not so endless. In the next moment, he separated his mouth from her own and set her back from him rather forcefully.

"You are the sweetest, most blameless of young women, Fontaine," he growled. "But I fear you've the wrong sort of Knight protecting you."

Fontaine cast timid eyes to the ground and, with one trembling hand, wiped at the moisture still clinging to her lips. She felt shy, discomfited. No doubt Knight was accustomed to women with far more experience and skill in matters of affection.

"I am...I am sorry my...my inexperience displeases you, Knight," she whispered, tears gathering in her eyes.

She gasped when she felt his hand none too tenderly take hold of her face, forcing her to look at him, the expression of frustration, of anger, on his face awing her to silence.

"Displease me?" he growled. Capturing her mouth once more, he kissed her fiercely, a pleasing brutality emanating from the force of it. He pulled her tightly to him, bound her in the strength of his arms. As his unyielding kiss sustained, his hands traveled to her hair, wrapping the tender tresses in his fists. He clutched her waist, held her head between the power of his hands, all the while his kiss steady, dominant.

When next he released her, he stood scowling, his sculpted chest rising and falling heavily with scarcely controlled breathing.

"A word of warning, peach," Knight growled. "Keep yourself from my company for a day…lest you find this circumstance of my being your lover far from being a farce!"

Fontaine held her breath until Knight had slammed the greenhouse door behind him. In his wake, he'd left her confused, enchanted, trembling, and alone with not but his discarded shirt and vest at her feet. And she was done for, the victim of her aunt's triumph. For now, more than ever before, she knew the rogue Knight—one moment sympathetic liberator, the next passionate lover—she knew he owned her heart. She knew he ever would.

Slowly her trembling hands gathered his discarded shirt and vest, drawing them to her face. She inhaled deeply of their scent, the scent that was her Knight—the scent of hickory smoke, shaving soap, and leather. Still, through her tears she smiled at the remembrance of his parting words to her. *Lest you find this circumstance of my being your lover far from being a farce*, he had warned. Was it preposterous to dream of his having enjoyed kissing her?

A demon he was! A scoundrel! An asinine ignoramus as well! To have thought he could touch the girl and remain in control of his desires for her—what fatal error had he made in his undertaking to help her? By giving into his want to taste of her kiss, he had jeopardized his entire purpose.

As he strode angrily toward the manor, he mumbled, rebuking, reprimanding himself for adding so seriously to the girl's corruption. He shook his head, cursing under his breath. She'd thought she'd displeased him. In his entire life he had never experienced such pleasure! He thought briefly of Annastice, of his once thick infatuation for her. Never had Annastice's kisses affected him so, caused him to wonder if he could leave her—but this girl. And he was a liar! Fontaine would loathe any and all liars, no matter what their reasons for deception.

Storming into the kitchen, he said nothing to Marta and Big William as they stood staring at him, eyebrows raised in astonishment at his lack of clothing.

"Keep her out of my reach for today, in the least of it!" he growled. "And bring me parchment, pen, and ink. I've a letter to write."

"He's one to be orderin' us about like he was lord of the manor, he is," Marta said to William once Knight had stormed out of the room.

William's eyes narrowed. "He's lost his footing, that one," he muttered. "The young miss is itching him under his skin."

Marta smiled, triumphantly nodding at William. "Let's hope he can't scratch it away too soon."

CHAPTER SEVEN

"It has not escaped me, Fontaine," Lady Wetherton began as the coach rumbled toward Lord Greenville's estate, "how much pleasure you tend to take in Knight's attentions of late."

Fontaine remained outwardly calm even though her innards were a torrent of turmoil. She'd never expected her aunt would mention her supposed affair with Knight. Though she saw no possibility of the woman's being able to question Knight's fulfillment of his obligation after witnessing the scene in the greenhouse several days earlier, she assumed her aunt meant to play ignorant of it. Thus, Lady Wetherton's remark as the coach drew near to Lord Greenville's estate, where his annual spring ball was being held, unnerved Fontaine.

"What woman wouldn't take pleasure in attention from such a man?" Fontaine managed.

Lady Wetherton raised one eyebrow. "True enough. Only...refrain from any flirtatious inclinations you might have toward him, my dear." Then again revealing her true character, she added, "At least, refrain from them in any public venue." So she had seen Knight's moments with Fontaine at the greenhouse. What other reason would she have for such conversation?

Fontaine sighed and gazed out the coach window. Lord Greenville's estate was in sight up ahead, and her stomach churned at the thought it.

"Men serve one of three purposes in life, Fontaine dearest," Lady Wetherton said. Fontaine rolled her eyes with irritation. She'd hoped her aunt had quitted the subject. "As a plaything, in the first. A way by which we, as the fairer gender, might entertain ourselves."

"Aunt!" Fontaine scolded. She had no wish to be privy to her aunt's opinions on the subject.

"Pray listen, niece…so that you may not be caught ignorant in matters of men," Lady Wetherton said, adjusting a thick, black ringlet at her temple.

Fontaine sighed, reconciled to enduring one of her aunt's lectures.

"In the second, they are oft necessary as a means to avoiding poverty," the lady continued. "Poverty should be avoided at any cost, Fontaine, for it is miserable beyond your ability to imagine misery."

Fontaine thought for a moment that poverty might be a sort of heaven as opposed to marriage to Lord Greenville. The contemplation of heaven led her thoughts to Knight. She was glad it wasn't raining, lest he be soaked to the skin while driving them to Lord Greenville's gathering. She smiled, feeling safer in knowing he led the team, which now carried her to her destination.

"I'm glad to see you agree with me in that, at least," Lady Wetherton said, misunderstanding Fontaine's pleased smile. "And lastly, if a woman were inclined to bear children—and I suppose it is good that some are, else humanity would discontinue altogether. Therefore, they are admittedly necessary to that process as well."

The coach entered the circle before the great oak doors of the Greenville manor, and Lady Wetherton concluded her lecture.

"Thus, know that I find no fault with your dalliance where Knight is concerned, Fontaine. I only warn you, for you must protect your place in society…at least until such time as your place in society is firm, my dear."

Fontaine closed her eyes for a moment, sickened by her aunt's selfish reasonings.

Knight opened the coach door, drew out the step, and offered his hand to Lady Wetherton. Once he'd assisted her in her exit of the conveyance, he held out his hand to Fontaine. She smiled and accepted, stepping from the coach.

Pausing, she looked up into the fire of Knight's eyes before following her aunt into Lord Greenville's manor. Since he'd kissed her in the greenhouse three days before, he'd seemed somewhat troubled and distant. Fontaine had sorely missed the brilliance of his smile, the warmth of his touch, his teasing manner. Further, she'd desperately longed to have his kiss once more. And so she was encouraged when he smiled at her and winking pressed a small slip of parchment into her hand.

"Have a wonderful evening, milady…Miss Fontaine," he said, nodding at Fontaine encouragingly.

"Thank you, Knight," Fontaine told him, warmed by his undisturbed gaze.

"Yes, Knight. Thank you," Lady Wetherton added. "Pray, Knight," she said, turning back to look at him then, "do not stray too far, in the case I should weary and wish to return to the manor prematurely."

"Yes, milady," he said with a respectful nod.

Fontaine could not find solitude quickly enough! She must see what was written on the parchment Knight had entrusted to her.

After allowing one of Lord Greenville's maids to take her cloak, she quickly unfolded the parchment, slowing her step.

10:00 p.m. In the coach, was all that was written upon it. Still it was enough to send her heart whirling into delirium at the prospect of such a secret meeting with Knight.

"Miss Fontaine," Lord Greenville greeted as Fontaine entered the ballroom. "How lovely you look in that blue frilly frock."

"Thank you, milord," Fontaine said with a curtsy. She forced a smile as she studied the man for a moment. At sixty and three, he was uglier than most dead men, she mused. His head was bald, save a few wiry gray strands of hair, which poked up about his ears like dog's whiskers. His lips were dry and red, and his tongue kept creeping out of his mouth to moisten them. Even as he bent to take her hand, she could smell the stench that was his breath. Mingled with the stench of his breath were the nauseating odors of wet woolens and old cats. There was something strange about a titled man who kept cats instead of dogs. Oh, Fontaine adored cats, but they seemed a lady's pet rather than a lord's—even an old lord's.

"Might I claim the first dance?" Lord Greenville asked.

Swallowing hard, Fontaine forced a smile and said, "Of course, Lord Greenville."

"And I the second?"

Fontaine turned, and her smile became sincere as she beheld Mr. Dennis, her solicitor.

"Mr. Dennis!" she exclaimed. "What a delight to see you."

"And you, Miss Pratina," Mr. Dennis said, smiling at her and taking her hand. Mr. Dennis was, in contrast to Lord Greenville, a rather middle-aged man with somewhat too much thick brown hair and a pair of round spectacles. As for his breath, the scent of it was indiscernible, a welcome difference to their host's.

"Excuse me, sir," a young, dark-haired maid said as she addressed Mr. Dennis. "This has just been delivered for you."

"Oh, thank you," Mr. Dennis said, accepting the item from the young woman. Fontaine noted it was a letter, conserved with red sealing wax, though she could not discern the design of the seal itself. "Pardon me, for a moment," Mr. Dennis said, adjusting his spectacles and wandering away as he broke the seal of the letter.

"Ah!" Lord Greenville said, taking Fontaine's hand. "The musicians have begun. Our dance awaits, Miss Fontaine."

Fontaine again forced a friendly smile, determined to endure, for at the stroke of ten, she would be with Knight!

The hours did not pass quickly enough. With each new dance, each new polite conversation, Fontaine grew more impatient. The enormous clock on the ballroom wall appeared to be slow, for it seemed days before it struck ten at long last.

As the clock struck the hour, Fontaine excused herself from the dreary conversation being held by her aunt and Lord Greenville. Neglecting to call for her cloak, lest her aunt's curiosity be stimulated, she hurried out the front doors of the manor and toward the bevy of coaches crowding the grounds.

It was terribly dark; still, she found the coach swiftly, smiling as she saw Knight leaning up against it, waiting for her. As she approached, he strode to her, took her hand, and led her back to the conveyance.

"We'll talk within," he whispered, glancing about in a manner of conspiracy before helping her into the coach. Climbing in after her, he closed the door behind them. Fontaine could not help but smile at him, excited by whatever reason he found to summon her to him.

"Mr. Dennis should be here forthright," he told her.

Fontaine felt her smile fade. She'd secretly hoped his reasons for wishing her to join him in the coach were more personal. "Mr. Dennis?" she asked, perplexed.

"Yes," Knight answered. "I've been communicating with him for the past several days by way of written correspondence, and I've asked him to meet us here tonight."

"But…why?" Fontaine still did not understand what business Knight had with her solicitor.

A triumphant smile spread across Knight's face, however. "I've done it, miss," he told her. "I've found a way to rescue you."

A tiny spark of hope began to flicker in Fontaine's bosom. "You have?" she said.

Knight nodded, reached out, and took her hands in his own. "I have," he confirmed. "I considered everything you've told me about your father's will, your aunt's guardianship—you should've taken care to bring your cloak, Fontaine," he said.

Fontaine shook her head, irritated he should cease in telling her of his plans merely for concern of her cloak. "It's of no consequence. Have you…have you discovered something in the terms of the will? Something to force my aunt to quit me?"

Knight sighed. "Not necessarily," he admitted. "However, I think the terms can be manipulated until such time as you are of the stated age to inherit and choose your own spouse."

"How?" Fontaine asked.

At that moment, there came a knock on the coach door, and Knight inquired, "Yes?"

"It is Mr. Dennis," came the solicitor's response.

Knight opened the door and gestured that the man should enter. Mr. Dennis quirked one curious eyebrow and looked from Fontaine to Knight and back again as he stepped into the coach and closed the door behind him.

"Thank you for meeting with us, Mr. Dennis," Knight said, offering the man his hand. "I am Knight."

Fontaine noted the way Mr. Dennis's eyes narrowed as he studied Knight for a moment. "Randall Dennis," Mr. Dennis said. "It is good to finally meet you…face to face, sir." Mr. Dennis turned his attention to Fontaine then. "Let me assure you, Miss Pratina…my loyalty has always been to you. Dealing with your aunt was only forced upon me by necessity."

"I know, Mr. Dennis," Fontaine said, smiling. "And I thank you for all you have done for me since my parents' deaths."

"As to the subject of…Mr. Knight's proposal…I pause, naturally," Mr. Dennis said.

"A wise man would," Knight assured him.

"Still, I know the kind of woman Lady Wetherton is, and I doubt not that your good friend Mr. Knight is correct in his theories of her intentions, for she has been to see me this very week, asking to witness the will again, asking about laws of marriage and inheritance," Mr. Dennis said. Fontaine frowned, felt panic begin to rise in her. "And, though it seems rather a bit extreme perhaps, I believe Mr. Knight's plan, as it were, may be the only way to preserve your inheritance…and you, Miss Pratina."

Mr. Dennis paused, removing several pieces of parchment from his coat pocket. "Therefore, it must needs be I obtain your signature on a few documents, miss…in that—"

"Perhaps, Mr. Dennis," Fontaine interrupted, "perhaps Mr. Knight would like to inform me as to his plan…the method by which he intends to preserve me." Her eyes narrowed. How could a solicitor so well-known for his ironclad knowledge of the law and unmatched loyalty be so easily swayed by a coachman? "And," she added, "I beg you, Mr. Dennis...what cause have you to entrust my welfare so completely into the hands of a man you have never before met?"

Knight felt an admiring grin spread across his face. He was pleased Fontaine would question her solicitor in such a manner, for these were odd circumstances indeed. He allowed his gaze to linger on the berry of her lips and could feel the rogue in him rising.

Mr. Dennis did not pause in his response. "I have made many inquiries into...Mr. Knight's past and character. Likewise, I have been in communication with those who endeavor to help him to help you. His connections are...very impressive and without blemish."

"You trust Knight then?" Fontaine asked. Her own feelings and her trust in Knight were one thing, but she was quite surprised he had won over Mr. Dennis with such apparent ease.

"I do, Miss Pratina," Mr. Dennis answered, "else I would not be here now."

"Mr. Dennis will play a part of his own," Knight interjected. "It will not be me who will be solely responsible for hiding you away."

So he did mean to spirit her away, to hide her. Fontaine's heart was aflutter, delighted by his willingness to help her with such desperate measures.

"Hide me where?" Fontaine asked. "And how will hiding me stop Aunt Wetherton's plans exactly? Of course, I will not physically be here; therefore, I suppose she will be unable to force me to marry. Still..."

"In truth, the entirety of it is reliant on interpretation of an article in your father's will, Miss Pratina," Mr. Dennis said. "I dared not bring it with me here tonight, but you may remember the exact wording of the marriage stipulation."

"I'm afraid I do not, Mr. Dennis," Fontaine admitted.

"It reads thus: 'In the matter of the marriage of our daughter, Fontaine Pratina, upon becoming Lady Wetherton's ward; before said ward reaches nineteen years, Lady Carileena Wetherton, whilst in the company of said ward, may choose of suitable and titled men one worthy of being wed to said ward. Further, said ward must conform to such a match.' " Mr. Dennis paused and then continued, "My interpretation—and being the current, elected executor of your father's will, the interpretation is mine to deduce—this particular specification causes me to state that if in fact Lady Wetherton is not in your company, she cannot force you to marry. This would leave you free to choose a husband once you reach the specified age…or before."

"Or before?" Fontaine asked, still stunned by Mr. Dennis's revelation.

"Yes," he said, "for the will further states, 'In the matter of the marriage of our daughter, Fontaine Pratina, upon becoming Lady Wetherton's ward; before said ward reaches the age of nineteen, said ward may marry only with the permission and consent of Lady Wetherton, assuming Lady Wetherton is capable of consent to the marriage. If Lady Wetherton is, for any legitimate reason, unable to provide consent, said ward may assent to her own marriage whereupon Lady Wetherton's guardianship of said ward is thus ended.'"

"Do you mean to say, all this time, I have had my choice of husband before me?" Fontaine asked. Anger was swelling in her throat. Why had Mr. Dennis not said something sooner?

"In truth, Miss Pratina," Mr. Dennis began, "you were but fifteen when your parents died. If you'll remember, these specifications seemed less pressing…at the time. Similarly, the stipulation, 'any legitimate reason'…in truth, Miss Pratina, your aunt could construe your running away, as it were, as far less than a legitimate reason, thereby evoking the article in the will stripping you of your inheritance completely."

"What do you mean?" Fontaine asked. Why would her parents include any such article in their will, which would strip her of her inheritance as punishment for marrying whomever she wished?

"My supposition is they wanted to ensure you wouldn't scuttle off with the first coachman who caught your fancy, miss," Knight said, winking at her.

"Exactly," Mr. Dennis confirmed. "As you know, I did not draw up your father's will, Miss Pratina. However, my father did, and he was a great one, unfortunately, for making certain an heir remembered to marry appropriately."

"Your capability to marry a man of your own choosing before your nineteenth birthday is not relevant, in any case," Knight said. "I simply intend to remove you from your aunt's presence, thus preventing her from exercising the rights of the first article on marriage in your father's will."

Fontaine swallowed the large lump in her throat. Hope in her was mingling quickly with fear.

"Where…where would I go?" she asked.

"It is being arranged," Mr. Dennis answered. "And your father's will goes before you. It is your choice to have it secured by whomever you wish. This way Lady Wetherton will have no access to it, no chance of destroying it, for there is no article in the will allowing her access to it without your presence. That has not changed since first I interpreted it," he explained. "I've contacted a close acquaintance, a fellow solicitor practicing in the same town where Knight will be taking you. Your father's will should be in his care promptly…once you've signed the papers authorizing my transfer of it, of course."

Fontaine's mind was whirling, stretching to comprehend all that was before her. "Mr. Dennis," she began, "you have been in correspondence with Knight these past days."

"Yes, miss," Mr. Dennis confirmed.

"And…and Knight has already proven his loyalty to me," she mumbled, more to herself than to anyone else.

Both men were silent, no doubt understanding the great decisions before her.

"I want nothing more than to escape the influence, the very presence, of my aunt," Fontaine said. "Still, to trust so completely…to place my welfare in…in…"

"In the hands of a near stranger," Knight finished for her.

"Yes," she admitted. "Where am I to go? How will I survive?"

"There is the amount you have put in trust with me, Miss Pratina," Mr. Dennis reminded.

"Oh yes," Fontaine breathed. She'd forgotten about the rather generous, but likewise limited, sum she'd nestled away over the past few years. Many times she'd taken the clothing allowances or gifts of tender on her birthday and holidays her aunt provided and placed the greater part of it in trust with Mr. Dennis.

"It is enough to see you through a modest existence, until you inherit," he explained.

"And I've arranged for your sanctuary…in the home of an elderly woman desirous of a young companion to keep her company,"

Knight explained. "She is the kindest of women," he added, "and will, no doubt, love you like a daughter."

"I see," Fontaine whispered, her hands wringing in her lap. It sounded so simple, the way they put it to her, but trepidation had gripped her, and she feared her courage might fail. "And…and when is this…when am I to leave?"

"There are still many arrangements to be made," Mr. Dennis said. "It may be some time yet, Miss Fontaine."

"Some time, you say. Are you meaning a month, two months?" Fontaine asked.

"Within four weeks, I would hope," Knight answered.

"Four?" Fontaine breathed.

"I must return to the gathering within, Miss Pratina," Mr. Dennis said. "One or the other of us might not be missed by your aunt. But both of us will. Please, linger here for a few minutes so we may return apart."

"Very well," Fontaine said.

Mr. Dennis took one of her trembling hands in his own and said, "It has always been one of my greatest wishes…to help you, Miss Pratina. I am glad your…your friend Knight is as wise as he is to involve me." Handing her the folded parchments he'd produced from his coat pocket, he said, "Sign these as soon as you are able, and Knight will have them delivered to me. They are legal tender allowing me to award possession of your father's will to Mr. Price Stantish, the solicitor I mentioned before." Mr. Dennis raised Fontaine's hand to his lips, kissing the back of it lightly. "Good luck to you, Miss Pratina. And should you ever need help, know I am willing to assist in whatever manner I am able," he said before leaving her alone in the coach with Knight.

Fontaine looked at the parchments in her hands. The entire plot seemed surreal! Insane! To run away with Knight to a strange residence, a life of hiding and secrecy? She glanced up to Knight. And what of Knight? Would he stay with her in her hiding? Or would he resume his traveling and leave her to her own, feeling his obligation to her met?

"I see you are wildly unsettled, miss," Knight said, his voice low and soothing in tone. "So much to absorb and contemplate. Still, I see no other way to remove you from the clutches of despair."

Fontaine drew in a deep breath and bravely straightened her posture. "I know you are correct, and your wisdom, your knowledge, is apparent in your actions. Your boldness, your ambition in plotting this all out, should not surprise me, and I am thankful for your strength…yet I feel somehow helpless and ignorant."

She gasped when he leaned forward suddenly, taking her face in his hands. "You are neither helpless nor ignorant, miss," he said, the emerald of his eyes burning even for the darkness of the coach. "You are, however, ensnared in a web…a web of your aunt's manipulation and cruel intentions. Thus, you are vulnerable and may fall victim to great disappointment, unhappiness, and harm. As a fish in the fisherman's net, you simply need help breaking your bonds. And I intend to help you, peach."

Fontaine sighed, a grand relief washing over her as she felt the warmth of his touch. Knight would keep her safe; her soul promised it. Taking the parchments from her and tucking them safely into his inside coat pocket, he covered his hands with her own, and she smiled up at him.

"I'll keep these with me until we are back at the manor and you are able to sign them," he said, patting his pocket.

Fontaine sighed, further confident in his ability to protect her. "What you've done, what you plan to do for me, sir," she began, "goes far and beyond fulfilling any obligation."

He smiled, and her heart began to beat wildly as his arms began to enfold her, pulling her closer to him. He moistened his lips, and his head descended toward hers. He meant to kiss her! She could see the intention in his expression, and her arms broke into gooseflesh at the anticipation of it.

"She…she cannot see us in here, Knight," Fontaine whispered, silently begging that he should kiss her just the same. "You are under no requirement to her to pay me such attention now."

Knight chuckled and kissed her lips lightly, whispering, "She could not see us in the greenhouse three days past, when I captured you, tasting of your sweet mouth then either, Fontaine."

Fontaine's jaw went loose, her mouth slightly agape in astonishment at his revelation. Her heart pounded madly with the knowledge he had kissed her—nay, made love to her—of his own volition, not for the sake of her aunt's watchful eye.

"And now," he mumbled, "a second delicious helping." His mouth found hers, moist, warm, refreshing. The passion Knight evoked in her burned over her flesh, caused her mind to be lost in the enjoyment of it, and she melted against him, accepting, returning his kiss fervently. The scent of him filled her senses, his touch causing her to tremble.

But he put her away from him all too soon. She glanced away shyly, afraid she had disappointed him in her eager acceptance and reply to his affections.

"Yet I must be measured in taking my pleasure, for I cannot send you back to Lord Greenville with your pretty mouth still moist and crimson from my attentions," he whispered, smiling. "Off you go," he said, opening the coach door, stepping out, and assisting her in her exit of it. "Before we are discovered."

Knight watched Fontaine hurry toward the manor house. *She is a sweet pastry,* he thought. He was unsettled by the pinching anxiety and distress in his chest as he thought of leaving her off with old Lady Lightender. In truth, his emotions where the Miss Fontaine Pratina was concerned were passionately unfamiliar to him. He thought again of Annastice, of what he'd known of matters of the heart with and through her. His feelings, his desires toward Fontaine were shamefully different, and he wondered how he could have reached such an age of twenty and four years ignorant of it all.

Again, the thought of leaving her once he'd secured her safety caused his stomach to churn, his head to ache, and his heart to pinch—for in fact, he wanted to keep her! It was only in that moment he let himself admit it. He wanted the Miss of Pratina Manor for himself. Visions of introducing her to his mother rattled around in his brain. Visions of little golden-haired daughters of his own, bred of a union between himself and his pretty peach, had winked at him of late through his dreams.

Perhaps he should simply tell her the truth, confess his true origins. But he knew what distain she would feel for the truth of it, and he would rather set her on a path to her own happiness than taint her any further with the truth that was in him.

"Are you indeed overheated, Fontaine?" Lady Wetherton asked as Fontaine stepped anew into Lord Greenville's ballroom. "Your cheeks are scarlet with a blush."

Fontaine shook her head and vanquished the smile from her face. "Yes. Indeed I was a bit warm. However, a quick breath of night air at the window has cooled me."

Lady Wetherton's eyes narrowed, her suspicious expression all too discernable. But Fontaine could not be made unhappy at that moment—not with the knowledge, the hope of escape. And certainly not with the sense of Knight's ardent kiss still clinging to her lips.

CHAPTER EIGHT

As the carriage approached The Graces, Fontaine felt her very soul sigh with happiness. In the two weeks since Lord Greenville's ball, since her meeting with Knight and Mr. Dennis in the coach, great hope had become mingled with great heartache. As she had further learned of Knight's preparations for her safety, so had she come to know her heart would break when the conspiracy was set in motion. She would well be safe from her aunt's selfish manipulations, but she would face her heart's death in losing Knight. Oh, he hadn't told her, hadn't verbally confirmed the fact he would be leaving her off with this Lady Lightender, then finding his own way, but she knew it to be true. It was in the way he never involved himself in the talk of the future once she'd arrived at her destination, in the way he looked at her rather guiltily at times.

Fontaine was nearly certain Knight cared for her deeply; whether as a sweet friend, a personal pet, or in any manner otherwise, she knew he cared for her. Their conversations of late had been filled with deep substance. His laughter and smile were gifted to her sincerely and easily enough, letting her know he at least liked her. And his affections! Oh, how blessedly she'd been lost in his affections! Her flesh prickled with delight at the memory of their most recent interlude.

Only the day before, as Fontaine had been on her way to the library, Knight had passed her in the hall, nodding and donning a mischievous grin. However, instead of passing her by, he'd reached out, taking hold of her arm and staying her. He'd glanced quickly about, ensuring their privacy, before pulling her into the linen closet with him. Oh, the scent of fresh linens, the flavor of sunlit wind still clinging to them—how that scent would ever remind her now of warm moments in Knight's arms, of the feel of his body against hers, of the sweet spice of his kisses.

Fontaine smiled at the memory, her body aching to be in Knight's arms, and misunderstanding her delighted smile, Lady Wetherton said, "Yes, niece. It is always preferable to dwell at The Graces, is it not?"

Fontaine couldn't stop the giggle that escaped her throat at her aunt's assumption that it was the sight of The Graces finding her smiling. And yet she did so love The Graces.

"Quite preferable, Aunt," Fontaine answered. "And look how lovely the lawns and hedges are already."

"Yes," Lady Wetherton said. "Daniel may not be the brightest of men…but his skill with the gardens is unmatched. I'm so glad I thought of sending him ahead early this year."

Perhaps it was because it had always been during the warmer seasons that Fontaine's family had dwelt at The Graces. Perhaps it was the sense of freedom and privacy country life afforded. Or perhaps it was simply because her parents had died at Pratina Manor. Whatever the reason, Fontaine always loved staying at The Graces. Had she had her way, she would never return to Pratina—simply spend all the year in the warm, safe loveliness of her father's country estate.

Knight helped Lady Wetherton and Fontaine alight from the coach. This country manor was far grander than the city one had been—all light and color against a clear blue sky. Knight understood why Fontaine's face seemed to pink up instantly, understood why her smile did not fade. And he was glad to see it, encouraged, for perhaps she would not feel so alone at Lady Lightender's estate. Though a great deal smaller, it held a similar charm and loveliness.

Knight had begun to worry in the days since first telling Fontaine of his plans to spirit her away. He'd begun to worry for her happiness. Yet he knew Lady Lightender was an amusing, pleasant old girl, not to mention her gardens were the things of dreams. Still, to abandon Fontaine, to leave her off with a stranger, it weighed on him. Further weight he carried with worrying for himself. Could he leave her? He'd begun to wonder if indeed he could release her from his heart, mind, and body wanting her so. However, each time he contemplated keeping her for his own, he was reminded that she would then know the truth. And he could not face the loathing that would no doubt fill her eyes at the sight of him then. Such lies he lived! Oh, the reasons for concocting them seemed justified at first meeting Fontaine, even somewhat necessary for her safety. Or so he'd thought at the time. But now, to tell her the truth, risk becoming the object of her scorn and resentment instead of the object of her affections—he'd rather lose her to happiness than lose her to hating him.

Yet he thought of her smile, her wit, her intelligence mingled with sweet innocence, and he wondered if he could leave her. The thought of her kisses, the softness of her skin further unsettled him. She had become as an intoxicator, an addiction to him, and he knew the only way he could leave her would be to return to his previous life—the life he was meant to lead, the life he hadn't known for near to two years. And perhaps now that life would look different to his more experienced eyes. Perhaps now he would learn to live it, swallow that it was his lot and unavoidable. Perhaps with as beautiful a memory as Miss Fontaine Pratina to keep his dreams company, he would even find joy in it—someday. Still, he doubted, for the set of circumstances was altered. Fontaine Pratina had altered them.

"Isn't it lovely, Knight?" Fontaine asked, smiling at him over her shoulder as she lifted her skirts and rather skipped up the front steps to The Graces.

He smiled, touched by the sheer joy of her expression. "Yes, miss," he said.

"Knight," Lady Wetherton said, returning to where he stood near the carriage, "may I see you in the library after dinner this evening?"

Knight felt every muscle in his body tense as she looked at him, again studying him from brow to boot.

"Of course, milady," he answered, nodding.

She nodded in return, and he knew: the time had come and far earlier than he had hoped. Lady Wetherton had seen the joy on her niece's face, her resplendence at being brought back to her beloved Graces, and the witch meant to destroy any and every happiness the girl had. Having returned to The Graces, an attentive lover in draw, Fontaine's joy must appear to her aunt as complete. And well Knight knew how unacceptable Fontaine's owning any delight was to Lady Wetherton. And since she couldn't simply strip away the existence of The Graces, she meant to strip away the only other thing the girl had: him. And so Knight knew—knew that this would be his last evening with sweet Fontaine. His very last. And he must make it extraordinary, a beloved, passionate memory that would serve them both in years to come. Serve them both in joy and heartache, perhaps, but serve them it would. He would make certain of it.

"Why she didn't send me to prepare the kitchens I'll never know, I won't," Marta grumbled as she hastened about the kitchens of The Graces, foraging for supplies with which to prepare dinner. "It goes to show where her priorities be, it does," she mumbled. "Oh! Send Daniel ahead so the gardens be the talk of the countryside. But ho-hum to the kitchen of The Graces! Let the neighbors gossip about how badly my kitchen is run."

Fontaine smiled, amused by Marta's dramatics. "Did you notice the pink hyacinth in bloom already, Marta?" Fontaine asked. "I could pick a basket of them and arrange a lovely centerpiece for the breakfast table tomorrow. Or perhaps Aunt Wetherton would allow us to bring out the pink rose china for dinner tonight, and I could—"

"Ya well know yar aunt won't hear of pink anythin' at dinner before April, ya do, lass," Marta reminded her.

"I do know it," Fontaine sighed. "But you wait and see, Marta," she continued. "When I am mistress of The Graces, we'll have pink rose china whenever we've a mind to."

"Blessed be the day The Graces has ya as its mistress, lassie," Marta sighed. "But who'll be the lord of it, miss? Tell me that."

Fontaine was thoughtful for a moment—rather depressingly so. "Perhaps there won't be a lord of The Graces, Marta," Fontaine said. "Perhaps my father was the last. Perhaps…perhaps I'll never marry…simply live out my days at The Graces, dreaming dreams of…of…"

"Of Knight," Marta finished. "Daydreams of Knight. That's a rather humorous way to think of it, it is. Daydreams of Knight."

"Hush, Marta!" Fontaine warned. "He'll hear you!"

"Don't ya mean to be sayin', 'She'll' hear me,' lass?" Marta's eyes danced with amusement.

"Of...of course that's what I meant, Marta," Fontaine stammered.

Marta sighed and sat down at the table across from Fontaine. "Why don't ya just confess it to him, lass? Tell the boy ya love him. Ask him to whisk ya away and to stay with ya forever."

"Marta!" Fontaine exclaimed, rising to her feet, her hands wringing nervously. "What a thing to say! You well know it is all a farce."

"I well know it is all *not*! That is what I know," Marta countered. "Don't let him vanish from yar life, lassie. Ya'll never recover from it, and that's just what she's wantin'."

The hot sting of tears irritated Fontaine's eyes. "He has his own life, Marta...his own agenda. Helping me has simply been the fulfillment of an obligation and—"

"Oh, posh!" Marta exclaimed. "I've seen the way ya two mingle up, I have," she said. "There aren't no farce there." Marta stood and walked to Fontaine. Placing her hands on Fontaine's shoulders, she looked into her eyes and said, "Ask him, lass. Ask him to keep ya with him, and see what he answers."

For a moment, Fontaine considered Marta's suggestion. Perhaps she should confess her love to Knight, confess she felt she might perish without him. Perhaps he would not leave her then. Perhaps he cared enough for her to...

"No, Marta," Fontaine said. "His agenda...his feelings are not the same as my own, and I will not heap guilt upon him. How would

I ever be happy wondering if he kept to me out of simple obligation? Or worse…pity?" When Marta only shook her head with disappointment, Fontaine explained further, "I…I sense he's akin to a wild horse…that he's ever cherished his freedom, his lack of being bound to any place or anyone. He'd choke being bound to someone who tried to tether him."

"Then ya don't know him as well as I thought ya did," Marta said. As her eyes narrowed, she added, "Or else…or else these are the things ya tell yarself to give ya comfort…to find the strength to let him go. That's it, isn't it, lass?"

Fontaine sighed and wiped a tear from her cheek. "I'll be in the garden, Marta. I'll arrange a few pink hyacinths for my chambers…if no one will have them at a table."

Quickly, Knight strode down the hall and into the library, his innards still trembling, the emotional result of the conversation he'd overheard between Fontaine and Marta. He was rather embarrassed of himself, not for eavesdropping but rather for being so deeply affected by what he'd heard and understood. His heart had taken to beating like a savage drum, perspiration gathering thick on his brow when he'd heard the two women mention his *keeping* Fontaine. And his heart beat wildly, his brow heavy with perspiration, not for fear of being *tethered* but for fear of the lack of it.

Perhaps he should just abduct the girl, carry her home, force her into marriage in the hopes she would forgive his falsehoods. The thought even crossed his mind, *I'll seduce her, corrupt her virtue, and her awareness to decency alone would find her willing to marry me.* But he would never bend to such lowness of deeds, even for the ache that had been growing harsher and harsher in center of his heart. He would never defile his beloved peach, body or spirit.

103

Knight closed his eyes, tried to calm his breathing, but this brought only vivid visions of Fontaine, of little golden-haired daughters and sons, born to him of her.

"I thought I had made it clear I wanted to speak to you *after* dinner, Knight," the witch said. Knight's eyes opened, a frown furrowing his brow as he saw Lady Wetherton rise from a nearby chair and move toward him. "Still, I suppose I should speak to you now. Why prolong the inevitable?"

"Milady?" Knight mumbled as he looked at the demon woman before him.

"The time has come, Knight," she explained plainly, "for you to quit my niece."

"I see," he said.

Lady Wetherton smiled a sickly smile. "You seem rather pale, Knight. Do not make pretense you have come to actually care for the chit."

Knight knew he must play the game carefully. Although his emotions were whirling about like a waterspout in him, he must be guarded.

"I only pity the young miss, milady," he said. "Lord Greenville is thrice her age and as ugly as the preacher's parrot."

Lady Wetherton laughed and, reaching up, caressed Knight's cheek with the back of her hand. Knight stood strong and still, resisting the temptation to take her hand in his vice's grip, crushing her bones to powder.

"So," she whispered, "you've guessed at my choice of a husband for Fontaine." Raising one eyebrow and caressing Knight's other cheek, she added, "Still, he is of great means, and she will want for nothing. So do not worry yourself too greatly over her well-being, sweet boy."

"When am I to end the charade?" Knight asked.

Lady Wetherton sighed. "Tomorrow," she said. "Quickly and unexpectedly. Let's not draw the pain out too long. You'll tell her tomorrow that you've...you've found other amusements." Lady Wetherton took one of Knight's hands in her own. "And I'll tell her two days hence of Lord Greenville's proposal. This will give her something to look forward to...something to ease the sting of losing her lover."

Knight forced an agreeing nod, understanding all too well the woman's intent—that the sting of losing her lover would only be increased a hundredfold by being told she was to wed Lord Greenville.

"Very well, milady," Knight mumbled. Then, reaching into his vest pocket, he withdrew a parchment.

"What's this?" Lady Wetherton said, smiling. She unfolded the parchment, and Knight watched her eyes narrow as she read it. "Your astuteness pleases me, Knight," she said. "We are more akin than even I thought."

"Yes, milady," he said. "And I will follow your instructions. I will quit the young miss...as soon as the parchment is signed and in my possession."

Knight had always known he would have to appear unaffected when the time came for Lady Wetherton to demand he break Fontaine's heart. And so he'd had a solicitor in the city draw up a legal article for the lady to sign, stating he was to be paid the sum originally promised him.

"I know milady would never falsely accuse," he told her. "Still, there is wisdom in my owning such a document stating I earned the sum and did not otherwise abscond with it."

Lady Wetherton laughed, obviously amused by his distrust in her. "Very well, Knight. Very well. You shall have the document back, complete with my signature, after dinner this evening. And tomorrow you will quit the chit. Agreed?"

"Agreed, milady," Knight said. Although he thought it impossible to do so, his loathing of the witch increased tenfold as she raised herself, kissing him lingeringly on one cheek before leaving him alone in the library. She wore too much rose scent, and her lips were cold and repulsive. If ever the poets envisioned a witch, Lady Carileena Wetherton was the embodiment of it.

Once Lady Wetherton had left the library, Knight slammed one powerful fist into the wood of a nearby bookshelf. Yet there was not time for anger. The witch had ended the charade two weeks earlier than Knight had hoped. And although the majority of the conspiracy's pieces were in place, there was still much to do. All the worse was the fact he must inform Fontaine of her aunt's hurried treachery. Still, Knight had no intention of quitting his lover in her darkest hour. The greater number of the times he'd stolen her away, whether for meaningful conversation or for significant hours spent rapt in passion, Fontaine's aunt had been quite unaware of their meeting. Yet the witch may be more watchful now, wanting to ensure the farce was quitted, her niece's young heart truly in tatters.

And so Knight resigned himself to careful progression. But he would make certain Fontaine knew it was careful progression and not adherence to her aunt's demands that would keep him at bay.

He would quicken his plans, make ready his accomplices, but it could wait. All of it could wait, for he would have Fontaine in his arms this night. *Yes*, he thought, the rogue in him swelling full ready, *I will have her for myself this night…the full length and breadth of it.*

The night was cool—overly cool to justify the window being open in Fontaine's bedchamber. Still, it was, for the scents and senses of the spring night at The Graces were meant to be savored, and Fontaine meant to savor them.

The last call of the meadowlarks was on the breeze billowing the window's lace curtains, and the sweet fragrance of hyacinth perfumed the room as well. Fontaine smiled, amused at the thought of having the window open whilst a fire burned warm in the hearth. Still, to Fontaine, this was spring—the time when temperature was in midpoint and fresh air was as needed as a fire's warmth.

Sighing, she snuggled beneath her bedding, anxious to take pleasure in the wonder of her first night back in the arms of The Graces. She closed her eyes, images of Knight begging to fill her dreams, and she listened—listened to the fire in the hearth, its familiar crackle soothing her. Listened to the breeze whispering through her window.

"Are you sleeping, peach?"

Fontaine gasped as she felt Knight's hand cover her mouth, felt his breath on her neck as he spoke.

"Shhh," he whispered, putting an index finger to his lips.

"Whatever are you doing, Knight?" she asked.

Knight brushed a lock of hair from Fontaine's forehead, and her body shivered with delight of his touch.

"I have come to ask..." he began, and Fontaine's eyes widened as Knight proceeded to climb onto the bed, stretching out beside her. "Are your wits about you, peach? Is your courage steadfast?"

"Wh...wh...why have you come to ask me these things?" she stammered, nervously distracted by the way he reached over her, letting his torso rest atop her own as he toyed with a long strand of her hair, the fire of his eyes flickering enchantingly in the firelight of the room.

"Because, I have been…this very afternoon…ordered to quit you," he said, placing a persistent kiss on her chin.

"What?" Fontaine exclaimed as panic pierced her heart. She tried to sit up, but the weight of Knight's body on her own prevented it.

"I'm to quit you, peach," he told her softly. "Tomorrow. And I've two years' wages in my pocket…making me a wealthy man, however momentarily, for we will make good use of your aunt's contribution to your escape. Still, being that I am, at this moment, a man of wealth…perhaps I may be deemed worthy of a night spent in your bed."

"Hush, Knight!" Fontaine exclaimed. "I cannot believe you would speak aloud such a thing as to imply…"

Knight's amused chuckling reminded her he was only in jest, and she smiled at him.

"Oh, how I enjoy seeing the astonished expression on your lovely face…that brief and fleeting moment before you realize I am in jest," he said. "Or…at least the moment before you *suppose* I am in jest."

Fontaine could not fight the temptation to reach up and place her hand to his cheek. He was so handsome! And such the true hero, her rescuer.

"I'll not have you spending all you've earned to my flight from her. The sum I have with Mr. Dennis will more than suffice expenses and…" she began, relishing the feel of his rough whiskers beneath her palm.

"Shhh," he whispered, frowning. "The sum is yours, in truth…for any gain she has comes from you, your inheritance."

Suddenly shy, Fontaine made to draw her hand from his cheek, but he caught it with his own, pressing her palm to his lips.

"And now for the details of the plot to extract you from your aunt's treacherous clutches," he said, rolling to his back and tucking his hands under his head. Fontaine scolded herself for delighting so in his proximity. His gestures—climbing into her bed, toying with her hair, and now simply staying beside her as they talked—were so very comforting and gave her great security, for the moment.

"Here is how the game is to be played, peach," he began. "Your trunks are already filled and readied, being we just arrived at The Graces today." He paused, frowned, and looked to her. "You haven't emptied your trunks as yet, have you?"

"No. Not yet," she told him, unable to keep from smiling at him.

"Good. In truth, it works to our benefit…her order that I should quit you. Your trunks are filled and ready to move. Big William and I, under pretense of helping Daniel haul away various and sundry garden debris, will load your trunks into the debris wagon, covering it with thick, thorn-infested garden rubble. I will then drive the wagon out to the woods—to unload the debris, naturally. However, a hired man and his conveyance will meet me in the woods, unseen…and will take your trunks all the way to Yoke Mortan."

"Then it is to Yoke Mortan I go," Fontaine whispered. She had heard of Yoke Mortan, its lovely country gardens and cottages. Somehow her fear of leaving, of going to a stranger's home, lightened a bit, replaced by an odd sense of adventure.

"Yes. To Yoke Mortan," Knight confirmed. He rolled onto his side then, resting his head on one hand, supported by his elbow. His eyes glowed with the fire of excitement as he continued, "Two days after your trunks have been delivered to the woods, so to speak…a coachman will arrive in those same woods and wait."

"Wait?" Fontaine urged.

"Yes, peach," Knight whispered, reaching out and twisting around one finger the ribbon securing her nightdress at her throat. "He will wait, while we, under the cover of night, of darkness, quit your aunt." He smiled at her and tugged at the ribbon, loosening the bow. "For our journey you will dress in mourning clothes, complete with thick, black veils. Therefore, if we are stopped or questioned for any casual or other reason, I will say you are in mourning…having lost your dear husband of late."

Fontaine swallowed, nervous of his toying with the bow of her nightdress.

Still, he continued, "It is one day's and half another's journey to Yoke Mortan, and we will take it in full. We will not stop for the night, for I do not want to risk discovery. Your aunt will have the constable and his hounds on us as quick as a cricket, so it is best we not stop."

Fontaine's hand went to the ribbon at her throat when one final tug from Knight's fingers caused it should unravel completely. He pushed her hand away and continued to twist the ribbon around his finger.

"And when we arrive at Yoke Mortan?" Fontaine asked. Oh, how she wished he would answer, *When we arrive, I shall whisk you off to nearest parsonage, marry you, and stay by your side forever.* But he did not answer it.

"When we arrive, I shall take you to a place much like this— Hunter's Bingham, the estate of my good friend Lady Penelope Lightender. She is elderly and in want of a young lady to keep her company and be her friend. I have written to her of you, and she cannot wait for you to come to her." Knight released the ribbon he had been toying with, letting his hand encircle Fontaine's throat in a tender manner of caressing her. "I trust her to keep you safe at Hunter's Bingham," he whispered, kissing her cheek tenderly.

"And you?" Fontaine could not resist asking. Already her senses were tingling with the thrill of his touch, the anticipation of receiving his kiss.

"What would you have me do, peach?" he whispered. "I may be recognized in Yoke Mortan, thereby endangering your hiding place." He pressed a gentle kiss to her lips. "Your aunt will be exceedingly driven to find you…and me. However, if I am found some way away from Yoke Mortan, what reason would she have to search for you there?"

Fontaine gasped in horror and took his face in her hands, searching his eyes with her own. "You mean to distract her? To serve as a decoy for my sake?" She had never imagined Knight would continue to place himself in jeopardy for her sake. What he said was sensible, yes, but likewise very dangerous.

"Of course, lover," he said, smiling. "Did you imagine otherwise?"

Suddenly Fontaine's mind, her heart could endure no more. She had agonized over the thought of giving him up to save herself, to avoid being married to Lord Greenville, to keep Marta and Big William, Daniel, and the other servants safe. But to know he would be at risk even after she was safely deposited in Yoke Mortan? To have him teasingly call her *lover*? It was too heartbreaking.

"You are to quit me, Knight. Then quit me!" she exclaimed in a whisper, tears filling her eyes. "For I am no lover to you and well we both know it."

"Do we?" he whispered, his thumb caressing the hollow of her throat.

Fontaine could no longer prevent the tears from escaping her eyes. "Come, Knight," she choked. "Do not make pretense you have conducted this *affair* with me in the same manner as you have those with your other, no doubt plentiful lovers of the past?"

His eyes narrowed as he looked at her, and Fontaine, humiliated by her inability to restrain her emotions, wiped angrily at the tears on her cheeks.

"No," he mumbled. "You are right…in part. However prejudiced in your assumption that I wander carelessly from lover to lover you may be…you are right in regard to the other." Fontaine cursed the prolific flow of tears that now traveled over her cheeks. "For one word from you, my peach," he whispered, his hand encircling her throat gently once more, "one word from you, and I would not quit you or your bedchamber this night."

"Ha!" Fontaine cried, the pain of heartache stinging her bosom. "Play the rogue all you wish, Knight, but I know you better than you think."

"Do you?" he whispered, caressing her cheek with the back of his hand.

"I do!" she exclaimed. "And were you truly the rogue you pretend to be, you would no more value my reputation, my safety, or my virtue any more than that of a common—"

Knight's hand over her mouth stilled her words. "One word, peach," he whispered, covering her upper body with his own as he gazed into her eyes. "Ask me. Say to me, 'My courage is failing me, Knight. Pray stay…keep me company this, our last, night as lovers.' Speak it, Fontaine…and I shall prove to you that I not only value your reputation, your safety, your virtue…but I shall confirm to you that I am protector to them. And to you." He brushed a tear from her cheek with his thumb.

Fontaine closed her eyes tightly. Should she resist? Push him away? On the morrow, he would be hers no more. Why lengthen the torture by keeping his company longer?

"Knight?" she whispered.

"Yes, peach?" he said, his voice low, deep, alluring.

"Knight…my…my courage is failing me. Pray—" she began.

But her voice was silenced by his mouth melting with her own. Desperation, the desire to hold him in her arms as long as she could, to kiss him, to have him kiss her—all of it was too unendurable, and she let her arms go around him, let her hands be lost in the softness of his hair.

After several long moments, he broke the seal of their kiss, stroking her hair as he gazed into her eyes and whispered, "I will not quit you this night, Fontaine. Nor will I quit your safety or virtue. But I mean to have the parts of you allowed me—your trust, your smile, the sound of your voice in my head as we talk." He brushed another tear from her cheek and kissed the spot, continuing, "The deep brown of your eyes, the feel of your skin on my palm, and the sweet taste of your kiss…those you will allow me this night. Will you not? Before I am made to quit you tomorrow?"

"Yes, Knight," Fontaine whispered.

Knight smiled, and Fontaine imagined there gathered moisture in the emerald of his eyes. "Not the rogue enough to disrespect and dishonor your virtue perhaps," he whispered. "Still, enough the rogue to intrude your bedchamber and draw pleasure from your lips."

Then, midst the perfume of spring's eventide, the passionate, heated kisses of the rogue, Knight, belonged to Fontaine…one last time.

CHAPTER NINE

The moonshine and starlight illuminated the shadowy spring night. The cool breeze carried the scent of wet grass into the coach, soothing Fontaine's anxiety a bit as she and Knight traveled through the dark toward Yoke Mortan. She marveled for a moment at how truly simple their escape had been. Save the rather long walk to the woods where Knight's hired coach and coachmen met them, there had been little difficulty in leaving.

The morning after Knight had explained his plot to her, the morning after he'd spent the entirety of the night in Fontaine's company and bedchamber exchanging conversation and kisses, Fontaine simply pretended to be overwrought with heartbreak whenever her aunt inquired of her. To her aunt's knowledge, Fontaine had never even left her room for the two days following Knight's supposed quitting her.

Each time Lady Wetherton would knock on Fontaine's bedchamber door, Fontaine would simply cry, "I…I am ill, Aunt. Please leave me to my miserable condition." This seemed enough to convince Lady Wetherton that Knight had completed his contract with her and to deter from further pressing Fontaine in any manner. Marta had explained to Fontaine how her aunt seemed quite radiant and delighted with herself, and Fontaine knew her aunt was basking in her supposed triumph at breaking Fontaine's heart and spirit. Furthermore, it had kept Lady Wetherton from finding the chance to inform Fontaine of her plans where Lord Greenville was concerned.

With things as they were, it had been easy enough to slip away into the cover of a spring's night the day before. Now darkness was upon them again, and Fontaine was on her way to Yoke Mortan, to this Lady Lightender, to a freedom of sorts. Yet it took every ounce of strength her body could muster to push thoughts of heartache and loneliness from her mind. With Knight's plan set in motion came the loss of him, and often Fontaine thought she might wither and die when the dreaded moment arrived she must bid him farewell. In fact, she well imagined herself bursting into tears and sobbing, throwing herself at his feet and begging him to take her with him, not to leave her behind.

So many times during their long coach ride she'd nearly lost her will to resist him, nearly thrown herself into his arms, confessing her unrivaled love for him and begging him to keep her. So many times she'd nearly done it. So many times, and she wondered if she would do it yet.

Knight seemed preoccupied, rather brooding in his own right. Fontaine assumed his manner was purely the result of the anxiety induced by acting out such a dangerous conspiracy. He had explained to her he would not rest easy until she was settled in with Lady Lightender and he was on his way, bait for any investigators her aunt might send.

Still, as she considered him, studied his proud and strong profile in the low lamplight within the coach, he looked much troubled, not simply anxious.

"Knight?" she asked, at last. "Are you well?"

"Of course," he mumbled, looking at her and rather forcing a smile. "Merely impatient to arrive."

"How long have we yet to travel?" she asked him.

"Four hours…my estimate from what Barnes told me at our last stop," he answered. He looked to her again and asked, "How are you feeling? Are you frightened still?"

Fontaine sighed. "Yes…but not as deeply as I was yesterday," she answered. "The farther I travel from Aunt Wetherton, the better I feel. And you? What are your thoughts?"

"My thoughts?" he asked. "My thoughts are this. By now your aunt has discovered you are missing and that, likewise, so is her traitorous coachman. By now she will be deciding what to do…search you out, returning you to The Graces and forcing you to marry Lord Greenville? Or will she wait, biding her time…allowing it all to play out and hoping you come to some dreadful end, some sad ruination? Perhaps she will trust in my corruption of you becoming so complete that the terms of the will fall to her benefit. Therefore, my thoughts are these: which will her evil heart choose as the most significant benefit to herself? To endeavor to ensure your utter and complete unhappiness by stripping you of me and giving you into Lord Greenville's hands? Or will she choose to let you go in contemplation of owning your fortune?"

Fontaine felt a cold chill travel through her body at the consideration of Knight's thoughts. And although her aunt existed many and many miles behind her, still she existed, and Fontaine too wondered which road she would choose. Which was stronger in the witch—hatred and loathing for her niece? Or the desire for wealth of her own?

Nearly an entire day had passed since the moment Lady Carileena Wetherton had been informed of Fontaine's disappearance—of Fontaine's and of Knight's. Sitting in the large chair in the library of The Graces, the lady considered on the situation. She could not accuse Knight of kidnapping or theft, for she herself had been ignorant enough to sign a parchment attesting to the truth of his being paid for the completion of a contract. Therefore, if she were to contact the constable, accuse Knight of kidnapping Fontaine, attempting to gain the help of the law to retain her, then she would be found out via her own signed confession of conspiracy.

The woman then screamed out with frustration! Her plans, all her plotting, all of it foiled! How hard she had worked to gain Lord Greenville's trust, to gain his alliance, convincing him that having such a young beauty as Fontaine for his own was far worth the price he would pay Lady Wetherton in return. Lord Greenville had finally agreed to gift Lady Wetherton half of all Fontaine's inheritance, once the girl was legally wed him and the Pratina fortune became his by the statutes of the law.

And now, now she could not even view the terms of her brother-in-law's will, for the young trollop had spirited that away as well! Still, she was certain she remembered the inheritance terms correctly, and if Fontaine had indeed run off to marry a simple coachman, the entire Pratina fortune then fell to her guardian. And being Fontaine's guardian, this meant the fortune would fall to Lady Carileena Wetherton.

Drawing in a breath of contemplation, the woman reflected. Perhaps she should reconsider her rage. Perhaps Fontaine had simply handed her aunt more than she had even hoped for. In truth, which was the brighter road? To see Fontaine miserable, gaining only half of all that was to be hers? Or to see Fontaine disappear altogether and gain everything that would have been hers?

With the freedom such a fortune would merit, suddenly, though greatly vexed at being tricked by an insipid adolescent and a coachman who was too handsome for anyone's good, suddenly Lady Wetherton found herself reevaluating the circumstances.

Yes! Perhaps the action to take was none—none other than ensuring Fontaine did fall prey to the stipulations of marriage and inheritance in her father's will. Perhaps the wisest thing to do was let the girl marry her miserable, poverty-bound coachman. After all, how long would two years' wages last?

A relieved, triumphant smile spread across Lady Wetherton's face as she studied the magnificent library of The Graces. Yes, she would wait—wait for Fontaine to ruin her chances of inheriting and all simply because a handsome coachman had caught her fancy. Her smile broadened, for after all, who had put the handsome coachman in her path in the first place?

Knight sighed, his expression softening into a sincere smile. "I've been a miserable traveling companion, haven't I?"

"You've much responsibility, much to worry about," she told him. "I am merely the pawn, while you are the one in danger...the one who must carry out this plan."

"Pray do not make me out too heroic, peach," he chuckled. "I am quite wicked, in truth."

Fontaine smiled at him and linked her arm through his. "Wicked men do not set free silly damsels without demanding recompense...of some sort or the other."

"I am wicked, all the same," he told her, the emerald of his eyes smoldering with emotion. "I only pray you never discover just how wicked."

Fontaine smiled at him, deciding to change the subject of their conversation. She would not allow him to linger on ill thoughts of himself. "Have you known Barnes long?" she asked. Barnes was the man who met her and Knight with the coach, in the woods near The Graces. He was a tall, dark, serious-looking man, dressed in black, his hat pulled down low over his brow.

"He is my..." Knight began. He seemed to seize himself, however, as if he'd nearly revealed a secret. "He has been my friend for many years, and I trust him unfailingly," he answered, finally.

"Is he continuing on with you?" Fontaine asked. "Once you've put me off in Yoke Mortan?" Oh, how she wished she would be continuing on with Knight. She unconsciously moved closer to him.

"He is...for a time," Knight confirmed.

Fontaine loathed Barnes for a moment, envious that he should remain with Knight.

"However," Knight continued, "I am not *putting* you off in Yoke Mortan, as you state it. I am *letting* you off in Yoke Mortan."

"I wish you would not let me off at all, Knight," Fontaine whispered. She could no longer restrain the thought from escaping and closed her eyes tightly, attempting to contain the tears, which wanted so badly to release.

Her eyes opened once more, however, when Knight took her chin in hand, forcing her to look up at him.

"Please do not tempt me, Fontaine," he angrily growled. "I must do what is best for you, and life with a wicked man, a man who does not deserve you in any regard...would not be best for you."

Tears spilled onto Fontaine's cheeks as she asked, "Why are you so wicked, Knight? What manner of things have you done to cause you to be termed wicked?"

"Many," he mumbled. Fontaine noted the way his gaze fell to her lips, his tongue moistening his own. "Particularly of late."

"I've seen none of these wicked things," she told him. His hand moved from her chin to caress her cheek, brushing at a tear. "I've seen only your compassion toward me, the great sacrifices you've made on my behalf."

"Sacrifices?" he chuckled. "What sacrifices? I've been paid two years' wages to have my thirst for you quenched by your kiss."

"Two years' wages that you promptly used to free me from my bleak future," she reminded him.

He smiled, brushing more tears from her cheeks with his thumb. "Are these tears for me then?" he whispered. "For you shouldn't waste them on such a rogue as I am, Fontaine." He did not kiss her but wrapped her in his arms, pulling her against the warmth of his powerful body. "You should rest now. Yoke Mortan and Lady Lightender are in four hours, and you have slept little these past days."

He would say no more to her, and she knew it, so she slipped her arms inside his cloak and around his waist. He had not moved to kiss her since the night he'd spent in her bedchamber, and she knew he would never kiss her again. It was his way of beginning to put a distance between them. Oh, perhaps he had been her lover, found himself enjoying her company and affections far more than he first intended, for she had sensed the sincerity in him. But it was the past now, and only the future lay ahead, and Fontaine reminded herself of her own voluntary submission to loving him, knowing he would be stripped away from her. And she would find joy in it, somehow. Joy mingled with unendurable pain perhaps, but joy all the same.

Knight squeezed his eyes tightly shut, a tear escaping down his cheek to be lost in the soft fragrance of Fontaine's hair as her head rested on his chest. How had he allowed this to go so far? How had he allowed himself to fall in love with her?

It had all seemed so simple weeks before—so simple to plan out the recompense of an obligation, manipulate the manipulative witch until he found a way to help her niece, and then act on it. He hadn't foreseen his becoming so attached to Fontaine. Or had he? He wondered as he felt her arms relax about him, an indication sleep had overtaken her at last. He wondered if, from the very beginning, from the moment he opened his eyes to find himself in the sickroom at Pratina Manor, a lovely young woman at his side—had he known then he would love her? If so, why did he lie to her? Her, of all those he'd met on his travels, why hadn't he told her the truth from the first moment? Simply because he understood her unspoken disapproving revulsion of his kind? Had that been the only reason? Perhaps he would never know why he had lied to her about so many things, but he had, and that was that. There was no mending such deception.

Oh, how desperately he wanted her, wanted to own her, hold her, love her! Wanted to see her eyes in those of his children. But she was better than he was, deserved better than him, and he would see her have it.

He inhaled deeply the scent of her hair, let his chin rest in its softness. How he wanted her mouth to his! How he wanted one last taste of her kiss! But the time had come to let her go, and one last kiss might be the end of his determination to save her. One last kiss might break his will to protect her, causing him to keep her, take her with him no matter the consequences. And for her sake, for the sake and safety of his lovely, delicious peach, he must find strength—an unselfish strength the like he had never been able to find in himself before.

Oh, but he loved her! How madly he loved her! How he would always love her—the deep brown of her eyes, the gold of her hair, her compassion, her beauty, her kiss.

Another tear escaped his eye, coming to rest atop her head, and he kissed her there, just where his tear had moistened her hair— kissed her again and again, softly as to not wake her. And Knight held Fontaine in his arms, safe in his arms, for the very last time.

"Oh, she's an angel, Knight!" Lady Lightender exclaimed, throwing her arms around Fontaine and hugging her tightly. "An angel!"

Fontaine could not help but smile as the woman released her, a resplendent smile on her lovely, wrinkled face.

"Yes, Penelope, she is," Knight chuckled. "Did the trunks—"

"Oh, yes, yes!" Lady Lightender interrupted. "Just yesterday, and they are safely tucked away in your chambers, love…all ready to welcome you to Hunter's Bingham."

"Thank you, Lady Lightender," Fontaine squeaked out, smiling at the woman's cheery face. Lady Lightender was herself an angel. White-haired and blue-eyed, her uncommonly rosy complexion gave her the look of a heavenly being indeed. Still, Fontaine's smile faded quickly, tears spilling from her eyes, for Knight would be gone. In another moment, she knew he would be gone.

"Oh, there, there, there, sweetheart," Lady Lightender cooed, wiping at Fontaine's tear-stained cheeks with the handkerchief in her hand. "It won't be so terribly bad as that. I'm a good conversationalist, well-versed in the poets and in the art of gossip."

Fontaine smiled through her tears at the woman's tender encouragements.

"I'll take my leave then, milady," Knight grumbled.

Fontaine forced herself to turn, to face him before he left. "Th...thank you, Knight," she choked. "For...for helping me."

Knight only nodded, and Fontaine noted the tight set of his jaw, the excess moisture in his eyes. Then, turning, he strode toward the door.

Please come back to me, Fontaine thought. *Come back to me...just once more.*

Then, as if his mind had somehow heard the silent thoughts of her mind and heart, Knight spun around, striding rather angrily toward her. Fontaine gasped as he took hold of her waist, pushing her back against the wall, his mouth descending to hers as if he meant to devour her entirely.

His kiss was driven and rough, yet exhilarating beyond description. Fontaine let her fingers weave themselves deeply through his hair, attempting to pull him closer, drink more deeply of his fiery kiss. He broke from her, his eyes locking with hers for a moment, both his chest and hers rising and falling with the labored breathing invoked of passion.

"Knight," she breathed, but any further utterance was silenced as his mouth took hers once more, drinking of her ardor for him with one last powerful kiss. And then he was gone, having released her and exiting Hunter's Bingham as swiftly as his long legs could carry him.

"Barnes!" she heard him shout as he slammed the door behind him.

"Oh my," Fontaine Lady Lightender exclaimed, obviously affected by what had just transpired before her. "I am beginning to think that, perhaps, Knight was not as forthcoming as he might have been in telling me his reasons for wanting to hide you away."

Fontaine tried to breathe, put her hand to her throat, attempting to remain conscious, for the pain, the utter ache wracking her body threatened to be the end of her.

"Sit down, darling," the woman said, taking Fontaine's arm and leading her to a nearby chair. "Murtle!" she called. "Murtle! A glass of water. Quickly!"

In another moment, an elderly maid appeared and handed a glass filled with water to Lady Lightender.

"Here, my sweet," Lady Lightender said, holding the glass to Fontaine's trembling lips. "Sip it slowly, and…and I've my salts just here." Lady Lightender waved a small glass vial under Fontaine's nose, and the bite of its scent indeed helped Fontaine to avoid a faint.

"I feel I might die," Fontaine sobbed as the sweet woman brushed the tears from her cheeks with a fresh handkerchief.

"Well, we can't have that, darling," Lady Lightender soothed. "We can't possibly have that, now can we?"

Fontaine's hands clutched the fabric of her bodice at her heart, her sobs irrepressible and aching.

"There, there, my love," Lady Lightender said. "You have your cry. You have it well, and then, my darling…then we will talk. Then we will sort this all out."

"There…there is nothing to sort out, milady," Fontaine sobbed. "Nothing!"

"My sweet, there is always something to sort out," Lady Lightender said, "especially where Desiderio is concerned."

"Who?" Fontaine asked. Was the woman mad? Had Knight left her in the care of some woman whose wits had left her?

But Lady Lightender smiled and said, "Desiderio. It means 'desired,' in his mother's native language. She prefers to call him Des."

The woman's appearance of delusions distracted Fontaine momentarily.

The woman smiled and brushed more tears from Fontaine's cheeks. "Desiderio Knight Lathan, my angel. That is his full and rightful name. One day the title of 'lord' will be added, when his dear father passes…but I hope that is far in the future. One day your Knight will be Lord Desiderio Knight Lathan."

"Forgive me, milady, but are you mad?" Fontaine asked, breathless with astonishment and lack of understanding.

Lady Lightender waved the vial of smelling salts under Fontaine's nose once more and continued, "Desiderio Knight Lathan, son of Lord and Lady Lathan of Lathan Green. Lord Lathan is himself a native of these parts. However, Lady Lathan hails from Spain. A true Spanish beauty she is; Knight has the true look of her."

Fontaine's eyes seemed to run dry, for her tears had quitted her cheeks, and she sat in awe at Lady Lightender's revelations. Could it be true?

"He is Knight…*only* Knight to me, Lady Lightender…a traveler…our…our coachman at The Graces," Fontaine stammered.

Lady Lightender nodded, raising an eyebrow as she said, "And well I was in agreement to let you continue to believe it…until I saw him fairly ravage you before my own eyes! Now I realize that my Knight has not been as forthcoming with me as he made pretense.

And thus I am inclined to investigate this matter further, to see what in the world he has been about this time."

"This time, milady?" Fontaine asked. She seemed unable to catch her breath, dizzy and fatigued.

"Murtle?" Fontaine heard Lady Lightender call out. "She's going after all, I'm afraid, Murtle. But perhaps it is best for now."

And with Lady Lightender's voice echoing the name of *Desiderio Knight Lathan* in her mind, consciousness was lost to Fontaine Pratina. Only a dark like that of night held her.

CHAPTER TEN

Fontaine felt fevered; full consciousness seemed elusive, for she could no more wake completely than she could make sense of Lady Lightender's strange revelations of Knight.

"Murtle," Lady Lightender's voice echoed, seeming far off and faint. "A cool cloth to her forehead should ease the perspiration."

"Knight?" Fontaine heard herself whisper. She was rapt in some odd sort of half-waking, half-sleeping dream where visions of Knight whirled about in her head, where his beloved voice sounded in her ears. And all at once, it seemed to her as if assorted and perplexing pieces of a puzzle began to fit together in her mind.

First she thought of Knight's proud posture, his frequent use of her common name, Fontaine, when speaking to her. These were definitely not traits of a well-weathered coachman. Then there was his unusual familiarity of the law and of interpretation of legal documents, his ease in contacting her solicitor and in so effortlessly gaining Mr. Dennis's trust. How suddenly he seemed to be able to hire a coachman and his coach, a man willing to involve himself in such a conspiracy as he had concocted. And then there was Lady Lightender herself. Why had it never before occurred to Fontaine to ask how Knight was able to secure her a position as companion to such a titled and wealthy woman? Even to his easy manipulation, his deep understanding, of her aunt, Lady Wetherton—even to his manner in playing the part of Fontaine's lover. Fontaine grimaced, her heart brutally aching as she admitted to herself then: no common man would've commanded such control over a wealthy heiress the way Knight had.

Tossing and turning, there was not else Fontaine could do, nothing but cry, heartache gripping her like the executioner's hand.

"And so," Lady Lightender explained, "Knight took his leave of Lathan Green…oh, nearly two years ago now. Weary of feeling ignorant to the plight of others who were less fortunate than he, he left intending to adventure, to discover and better understand the life of a common man." Lady Lightender smiled at Fontaine and held the glass of warm nutmeg milk to her lips. "Here, dear," she said. "Sip this. It will soothe you."

"I'm afraid little will serve to soothe me this night, milady," Fontaine said. For the past hour, Lady Lightender had sat at Fontaine's bedside, calmly relating the story, the adventures of this Desiderio Knight Lathan, son and heir of Legendar Lathan, wealthy lord of Lathan Green.

"Well," Fontaine said, a tear trickling down her face, "if he thinks he succeeded in actually living the life of a common man, as it were…then he failed miserably."

"Because of you, my dear?" Lady Lightender asked.

"How many ignorant, pampered young women of society foolishly lose their hearts to their roguish coachmen, milady?" Fontaine sniffled.

"Many more than you might think, I assure you," the elderly woman chuckled. "You know, dear…I was myself quite dumbfounded when Knight first wrote to me of your situation and his plan to extract you from it. For as noble, as honorable, and, yes, as chivalrous as he has ever been…I have never known him to act quite so recklessly, so…well, so desperately as this."

"He felt he owed me a great debt," Fontaine explained, wiping her eyes with her handkerchief. "He only meant to repay—"

"Oh, stuff and nonsense, child!" Lady Lightender exclaimed. "He's in love with you! Had he not been so completely smitten, so undeniably in love…he would've simply handed you an exorbitant amount of tender and hired someone else to help you!"

Fontaine shook her head, her tears increasing in their quantity. "Pray do not speak so, simply to try and make me feel the better, milady."

"And why do you not believe it, sweetheart?" the lady asked. "Why do you find it so very hard to trust in the truth…that he loves you madly?"

For all their conversation—for all Lady Lightender's explanation of Knight, his ways, his character, his reasons—one thing Fontaine could not deny, and she said, "If he loved me as you claim, Lady Lightender…then…then why abandon me? Why leave me off instead of taking me with him?"

Lady Lightender smiled. "Because, my precious, he is far too apt to hate himself, far too easy in thinking he is unworthy of beauty and love. 'Tis why he put off Lathan Green in the first place. He felt unworthy to govern the servants, the tenants, the townspeople. He feared the arrogance, the ignorance of the aristocracy he was born to. Why did he not take you with him, you ask me?" Lady Lightender smiled and produced a piece of parchment from the pocket of her sewing apron. "He has deemed himself unworthy of you, my darling." Holding the parchment out to Fontaine, Lady Lightender nodded.

"Read it just there, as I've folded it, dear. That is the part you need to read now," she said.

Fontaine brushed the tears from her cheeks and drew in a hurting breath, for even breathing had become painful, so completely was her heart breaking. Holding the parchment nearer to the lamp at her bedside table, she read:

…and so, my sweet Lady Lightender, I ask you to take what I cannot…the one thing I cherish above all else, including my own safety, my own life.

Oh, it is well I know you, my dearest Lady. You would have me confess my heart to the girl, sweep her away in my arms to Lathan Green, smother the breath from her with the passion burning so violently in me. But as the Lord doth hate a liar…so, I know, does Miss Fontaine Pratina. I do not doubt in her kindness, her willingness, and even her ability to forgive me my transgressions of deceit, and they are many where she is concerned. Still, I know it would change her toward me. I would lose her trust, her respect, and never gain her heart fully.

I am resigned then to return to Lathan Green, to take up my responsibilities, my position, leaving my treasure in your care until such time as she is nineteen and can legally escape the bonds that bind her so stiffly now. I would as soon kill this Lord Greenville as to see him lay a hand on my love! And being I do not wish to disappoint Fontaine further, or spend my remaining life in the black tomb of a prison, I feel it is best to simply spirit her away and into your care.

Lady Lightender reached out, taking the letter from Fontaine. "In its entirety, the letter is a lengthy exposition, to say the least. And when this chaos is put behind us all, you may wish to wade through the details he gives of his plan and how he intended to initiate it all. But for now, you have what you need to know to act as you should."

Fontaine could not breathe! She had read the letter, seen the confession in Knight's own hand. He loved her!

"And...and how is it that I should act, milady?" Fontaine asked. "He has put me off here. And further if my aunt finds me...if she should find Knight..."

"Believe in his love for you, my pudding, for it is truth," Lady Lightender said, returning the letter to her apron pocket. "I know I needed no further proof than his actions just this morning before he left. By all that is good I thought he meant to...to tarnish your virtue right there in my front entrance! I hadn't understood, I suppose, how terribly in love with you he is. Words are one thing, my dear; witnessing boldly displayed passion is quite another. Furthermore, I know exactly how you should act."

"You...you do?" Fontaine stammered, for her mind, heart, and soul were so tired, so tormented, so torn, she knew not how to rise from the bed, let alone act any further. In the space of two days, she'd gone from the familiarity of The Graces and its inhabitants, whether beloved or otherwise, to this Hunter's Bingham and its sweet, well-meaning Lady Lightender. Further, she was astonished at how quickly she'd fallen into intimacy with the great and kind lady. It was an odd feeling, to sit with a complete stranger revealing the deepest feelings of her heart. Yet the lady seemed known to her spirit, as if Fontaine had always known her.

"Indeed. I do," the woman confirmed. Then reaching out and taking one of Fontaine's hands in her own, Lady Lightender's eyes narrowed, and she asked, "How desperately do you love him, dear heart? What would you be willing to do to have him?"

Fontaine's tears began anew. "Any...anything!" she admitted in a whisper.

"Even forgive him?" the lady asked.

Fontaine shook her head. "It still escapes my understanding how he could think I would find him so vile, so unforgivable for his manner of deceit—after all he has meant to me, done for me. How could he think I would abhor him for his deceptions, the very deceptions that find me safe this moment, out of my aunt's calculating reach?"

"He told you many a falsehood, darling. Many a falsehood," said Lady Lightender.

"But...but if what you say is accurate, if this letter from him is strictly in earnest, the true reflection of his feelings...then who am I to be angry for it? For, in truth, I myself am a deceiver—out of consequence, the need to survive my aunt's insufferable character...or rather, lack of character. I've lied to her, played her game misleadingly. Even for frantic want of Knight's attentions...I was willing to deceive him, secret my love for him, from him that I love. I've run away, for mercy's sake! How can he not see the similarity in that?"

Lady Lightender sighed. "Knight was ever too critical of himself...ever certain he was unworthy. It's the very reason he left Lathan Green. Still," she said, standing and clasping her hands together, "it's time he had his comeuppance."

"Forgive me, milady," Fontaine said. "Fatigue, fear, despair, and so many other emotions have left my brain weak. What do you mean?"

"Did you know, sweet one…that I was Knight's Grandmother Lathan's dearest friend?" she said.

"No," Fontaine replied. How could she possibly know it? She'd only spent eight hours of her life in the woman's company.

"Well, I was," Lady Lightender confirmed. "Madalina and I were always in some sort of mess as children. You see, she had Knight's spirit, his talent for finding himself in a trick. Having said that, leave it to me." She started to leave the room but turned back to Fontaine a moment. "We'll let him stew in his own juices for a few days, love. Let him reflect on his decision not to confess all to you. Besides, I'll need the time to arrange things with Esperanza."

"Esperanza, milady?" Fontaine asked. "And…and time to arrange what?"

But Lady Penelope Lightender only smiled. "Oh, you'll see soon enough," she said. "And rest now. Rest knowing that in a few days time, you shall be in Knight's arms again, pretty girl."

However, rest did not easily come to Fontaine that night. Her mind was wildly tormented with the events, the discoveries of the day. Could it be? Could he truly love her the way his letter to Lady Lightender had indicated? Fontaine paused to believe it, worried that her mind had become diseased from heartache and was not in a rational state. Still, her body ached to be in Knight's arms, held close to the strength and protection of his body, and she could not keep hope from rising in her.

It was insanity! The whole of it was mad! The handsome son of a distant lord, masquerading as a common coachman, wooing and winning the heart of a young woman, the orphaned daughter of a

135

deceased nobleman. And then, to snatch the young woman away from the grasp of a manipulative, cruel-hearted guardian, deliver her into the hands of a secret friend, a noblewoman—who, at the first sight of the young woman, turns traitor to the nobleman's son, vanquishing his wishes of continued secrecy in order to help the young woman win back her coachman.

Fontaine's head spun with the confusion, to dream of it all, until sleep became her mind's only escape. Even then Fontaine dreamt of Knight, of his handsome face, his moist, heated kisses. As always, sleep brought Knight.

Knight lay in the large, comfortable bed of his chambers at Lathan Green. The artistry of the carvings on the ceilings of his chamber far surpassed those of the sickroom at Pratina. Still, though he did not miss Big William's boisterous snoring, he did miss the small sickroom at the manor—the room where he'd first seen Fontaine.

His father was away from Lathan Green, not in attendance when Knight had returned home late that evening. Still, his mother, Lady Esperanza Lathan, had burst into tears of joy upon seeing him. He thought of how even more beautiful she looked to him, her black hair, blue eyes, and loving smile tearing at his heart as she threw herself into his arms, sobbing into his shoulder.

What a fool he was to have abandoned his beloved mother as he did, in search of experience and knowledge. It seemed he was doomed to abandon the women he loved, and this gave him further testament in his wisdom at leaving Fontaine off with Lady Lightender. He grimaced at the thought of her, however, pain stabbing at his heart like a butcher's best blade. Closing his eyes, he inhaled deeply, hoping to find some hint of the scent of her. But there was none, only the scent of the linens on his bed, void of any fragrance to remind him of his sweet, delicious peach.

He could see her then, with his mind's eye—see her smile, her golden tresses, the deep brown of her eyes. His arms ached to hold her, protect her, feel the warmth of her body against his own. His thirst for her kiss gave him cause to grind his teeth in frustration. And he knew he would never recover—never hold the same excitement, the same bright hope of happiness in life he held before he'd awakened to find himself convalescing in a strange manor, his lovely Fontaine at his side. Without Fontaine, he would never again be complete.

Knight sighed heavily, attempting to recall the flavor of her kiss to his mouth, longing to taste her again.

Whom will she marry when she is nineteen, old enough to choose a mate? his traitorous mind whispered inside his head. *What fortunate man will have her for his own?*

Growling to chase away the appalling thoughts echoing through his brain, Knight rose from his bed. A midnight ride in the cool of spring's dark night would serve him better than the haunting thoughts his bed evoked. He would quit his chamber until the sun rose. Perhaps the bright of day's light would keep his longing for Fontaine's company at bay.

But even as he mounted his bay stallion, even as he rode through the mist of night's breath, he knew: Knight knew nothing would save him from the pain of losing the only woman he would ever love.

CHAPTER ELEVEN

"From the moment he stepped through the doors of Lathan Green, I sensed his unrest, his pain," Lady Esperanza Lathan said as she tied Fontaine's apron at the back. "I knew something was wrong...but he would not tell me what it was."

Three days had passed since Knight had given Fontaine to Lady Lightender—three days that Lady Lightender used to concoct her own conspiracy, her plan to reunite Fontaine with her beloved Knight.

Certainly Fontaine had been anxious, worried since the moment Lady Lightender had explained her plan to her. Still, it seemed such a long time since Fontaine had known anything save anxious worry, she wondered if she would ever again be able to experience other emotions. But Lady Lightender assured her she would. Therefore, for love of Knight and for want of his love in return, Fontaine had agreed to Lady Lightender's rather ironic scheming.

"I've received an answer to my letter to Knight's mother, Lady Lathan," Lady Lightender had explained the day before. "She is greatly relieved to not only know the reasons for her son's despondency, his inability to sleep since his return, but also to know of your existence. And she is in full willing, and I might add excited, to join in the conspiracy with us."

And now Fontaine stood in the Lady Lathan's chambers, the lady of the manor herself straightening the apron of Fontaine's maid uniform.

"He'll most likely drop dead, I'm quite afraid," Lady Lathan smiling said as she studied Fontaine for a moment. She winked at her next, and Fontaine noted how the charming roll of her Spanish accent complemented her great loveliness. Knight had the masculine adaptation of his mother's beauty, and Fontaine had relaxed just a bit upon meeting her earlier in the day.

"It is no wonder I find my Des so unhappy," Lady Lathan said, reaching up and straightening Fontaine's ruffled maid's cap. The lovely woman twisted a tendril of Fontaine's hair around her finger, tucking it quickly behind her ear.

"Well, it's all nonsense, Esperanza," Lady Lightender said. "Gone two years, and what did he learn of life? Nothing! Nothing but to deny himself the one thing in life that matters most."

"He is a stubborn, silly boy, my Des," Lady Lathan sighed. "But that is why you have come, Fontaine…to grow him up…make his happiness."

Every inch of Fontaine's body was trembling! She'd been unable to eat all day for fear of what was to come.

"What if…what if he becomes so angry with me that…what if you are both mistaken in your estimation of his feelings?" Fontaine stammered. To have him leave her off with Lady Lightender had been painful almost beyond endurance. What if he rejected her now altogether? It would be the end of her; of that Fontaine was certain.

"Oh, he'll be angry enough for the devil himself to fear him," Lady Lathan said. "But in the next moment you will be in his arms, and then…then he will be making love to you forever!"

Fontaine tried to believe the Spanish beauty's dramatic goings-on, tried to draw encouragement from Lady Lightender's affirming nod.

"I shall have to pull you from his embrace, spank him soundly on the seat of his breeches, and remind him that I raised him up to be a gentleman." Taking hold of Fontaine's shoulders then, Lady Lathan turned her around to gaze at herself in the mirror.

"You see!" Lady Lathan exclaimed. "The prettiest maid to ever grace the halls of Lathan Green."

Fontaine smiled, pleased by her appearance. She'd never considered herself in a maid's uniform before, and it delighted her, for now the tables had indeed turned. If Knight had played at being a coachman, she surely could play at being a maid.

"A wager, Esperanza?" Lady Lightender giggled. "I say he pauses, astonished into silence and confusion."

Lady Lathan giggled too. "I say he pounces on her as a cat on a mouse."

"I…I think he may be far too infuriated to be rational," Fontaine offered. "What if he picks me up by my hair and tosses me out into the gardens?"

Lady Lathan and Lady Lightender looked at one another for a moment. "Well," Lady Lathan sighed at last, "we do have lovely gardens at Lathan Green." When Fontaine's brow puckered with a frightened frown, both the Lady Lathan and the Lady Lightender fairly erupted into giggles, and Fontaine was somewhat relieved.

She considered the women for a moment, amazed at their ease of manner, their lighthearted ways. For the past few years, she'd known only her aunt's wicked manner, selfish and evil ways, and she began to remember that not all of those blessed with title and wealth were of the same measure of her aunt and Lord Greenville.

"Now," Lady Lathan said in a whisper, "he'll be ringing for his afternoon refreshment at any moment, and here is what you must do—"

"You must enter calmly," Lady Lightender interrupted.

"Yes," Lady Lathan agreed. "Enter calmly; set the tray at his desk, and when he says, 'Thank you,' you respond, 'Of course, Master Desiderio.' Are you able to do that, do you think?"

Fontaine put a hand to her stomach, which was churning with apprehension. "If I am able to stay conscious long enough," she said. Then shaking her head, she added, "He'll be enraged!"

"I've brought my walking stick just in that case," Lady Lightender assured her, holding her walking stick tightly in her fist.

Fontaine smiled at her, encouraged by her support. Again she wondered how it could be that she fell so easily into friendship with these strangers of late. It was unthinkable. Yet perhaps that was what loving Knight afforded: others in addition to himself who were of a fine, friendly, caring material.

"Are you ready then, my darling?" Lady Lathan asked.

Fontaine inhaled deeply and nodded.

All three women stood in the kitchen staring anxiously at the summoning bells on the wall. At last, the cord of the middlemost bell began to move, the bell ringing loudly.

"It's the study bell," Lady Lathan confirmed. "Quickly now, darling," she said, handing a silver serving tray to Fontaine and setting a glass of water and plate of cake on it. "Go to him." Lady Lathan put a soft, scented palm to Fontaine's cheek, smiling with encouragement. "And do not fear him, my dear," she whispered. "You're all he wants in the world. I promise."

Tentatively, Fontaine pushed open the door leading to Knight's father's study. Sitting at a large desk in the middle of the room, Knight seemed completely distracted by whatever document he was penning at the moment. Fontaine's heart nearly stopped at the sight of him. He was magnificent! She'd almost forgotten how magnificent! Tears welled in her eyes, and it took every bit of strength and courage she could muster to walk into the room.

Without looking up, he gestured with one hand that she should enter. "Pray set the tray here, miss," he mumbled, pointing to his desk. Fontaine stumbled once as she approached him. "Careful of the rug," he said.

She was standing directly next to him; she could smell the scent of leather and shaving soap—the familiar scent of him that she loved. Carefully, for her hands were trembling, she set the tray on his desk in the spot he had indicated and dropped a quick curtsy.

"Thank you," he mumbled.

Fontaine swallowed the lump of nerves in her throat and said, "Of course, Master Desiderio."

But he did not move, did not seem to recognize her voice, and with great disappointment and despair rising in her bosom, Fontaine turned, hurrying quickly across the room.

"Wait!" he fairly shouted. Fontaine stopped, her heart beating madly in her chest. "Come here, girl," he ordered, and she could hear the anxiety in his voice. Slowly she turned around, raising her head to meet his curious gaze.

Instantly his eyes blazed, the emerald of their fire piercing her very soul, and Fontaine gasped as Knight, frowning, took no time to circumvent his desk, simply stepping onto and over it, striding toward her like a starving panther.

She had not a moment to think, to consider anything, for the very instant he was close enough, Knight reached out, taking her throat in one hand and pulling the maid's cap from her head with the other as his mouth attacked her own with a driven, ravenous thirst.

"Fontaine," he breathed, his mouth leaving hers only long enough for his eyes to caress her face, the expression of wanton passion in his countenance. "Fontaine," he fairly moaned as he gathered her into the power of his arms, ravaging her with heated, moist affections.

Fontaine bathed in his embrace, returned his ardent kiss, let her fingers be lost in the softness of his hair. She took his face in her own hands, reveling in the sensation of his jaw working to enhance the passion between them, the intense passion threatening to rage beyond their control. And she sensed something new in him, an absence of restraint, and it thrilled rather than frightened her. She fisted her hands in his hair as he endeavored to hold her more tightly, drink more deeply of the flavor of her kiss.

"You must be properly wed before I can allow this to go any further, Des," Lady Lathan said firmly. And when he did not release Fontaine, Lady Lightender knocked the floor twice hard with her formidable walking stick. "Des!" Lady Lathan scolded.

Seeming rather winded, Knight indeed broke the seal of their kiss, gently pushing Fontaine from his arms.

Wiping the moisture from his lips, evidence of a passionate exchange, he said, "Mother…what have you done?"

"I've won a wager, Des," Lady Lathan said.

Fontaine noted the deep furrow that wrinkled Knight's brow, noticed the way he kept his eyes cast down toward the floor rather than looking at her, his mother, or Lady Lightender.

"You've ruined me," he mumbled. "And her."

"Oh, I do not think there is much ruin here," Lady Lathan said, looking to Fontaine and winking. "Simply two liars who need to repent." With that, she and Lady Lightender took their leave of the study, closing the door behind them.

"I'm trusting her to your care, Des," Lady Lathan called from beyond the doors. "To your care…and to your honor."

Fontaine would've smiled at the woman's rather amusing counsel but for the fact Knight did not seem to find it amusing. He had turned from her, his shoulders slumped in an unfamiliar manner of defeat.

"Why have you come here?" he growled.

Fontaine's mind reeled with confusion. Had he not, only the moment before, seemed jubilant to see her? And now, now he turned from her as if repulsed by her presence. What had begun as joy, joy in seeing him again, joy in his apparent caring for her, began to wilt into fear and heartache once more.

"Why…why did you leave me?" she whispered.

Whirling around, he glared angrily at her. "For your own well-being, Fontaine! For your safety! You know why! To protect you! To protect you from Lady Wetherton…and…and from me…a villain and a liar."

"You don't own the sin of deception, Knight," Fontaine cried. "And it is no good reason to quit me if you…if you really…"

"If I really love you?" he finished. His expression was so angry, so guilt-ridden, and Fontaine stumbled backward, stunned by what else she thought she read in him. "Do you think I am in love with you, Fontaine?"

"I…I…I hoped," she whispered as tears streamed down her face.

"Do you think you are in love with me?" he asked.

"I…I…" she could only stammer. Had his letter to Lady Lightender been a lie as well? His kiss only moments before, his ravaging of her, had it too been misunderstood?

"Then if I am in love with you," he said, reaching out and taking hold of her arm, "why would I bring you here—to risk discovery, to lead you into danger—when I could leave you tucked neatly away in safety and secret with Lady Lightender?"

Fontaine put a hand to her temple, for the pain there and in the rest of her head was becoming unbearable. "Then…then you are loath to think of me as anything but—"

"I am loath to think of you marrying Lord Greenville!" he shouted. "You forget yourself, Fontaine! You are but eighteen yet and have no verifiable reason to keep your aunt from forcing you to marry!"

Fontaine let her body fall back against the wall behind her and clamped her hand over her mouth as he continued in his shouting.

"The only way I can save you, Fontaine, is to…is to…" he began to stammer. "If I were to do anything else, if I were to myself take you to my…"

Suddenly, Fontaine recognized his raving as being the result of fear, not anger. And she knew, in that moment she knew what he feared. He wasn't afraid for her but of her. For what had Mr. Dennis's interpretation of her father's will been? Had not her father included an article in the will stipulating the consequences should she marry without her aunt's permission and consent before the age of nineteen? Yes, it was true. Should she marry under such

146

circumstance, she would lose her inheritance. And although she had borne great concern, wanting to acquire The Graces, to secure the futures of her beloved Marta, Big William, and the others, that was before Knight's appearance at Pratina Manor one cold winter's night. Fontaine realized in that brief moment how little it all mattered now, her father's wealth.

The article had been written as a protection against her marrying a common man and being left penniless. And what for it? Had Knight truly been a coachman, had she quit her inheritance and property to marry him, she knew in her heart she would be happier than ever she had imagined. She knew in that moment—sensed she had always known it—that coachman or heir to a title and great wealth, Knight was all she wanted.

And so she said softly, "I fully and freely forgive you, Knight." She watched him grimace as if someone had just plunged a knife into his chest. "Necessity...or fear...has made deceivers of us both. In truth, there is nothing I need forgive. Unless...unless you truly care nothing for me."

He stood silent, hands fisted, jaw firmly set, and, yes, moisture plentiful in his eyes. Fontaine's heart began to beat easier, despair melting from her soul as she studied him. "This...all of this, Knight," she began. "All of this was conceived in your mind when you first met me...before we played at being lovers, when I had no way of escape, no one to rescue me from Lady Wetherton's power, when it was necessary for my very survival to inherit my father's fortune, that I might have means of existing. And now, because of your false representation of yourself when first we came together, and your continuation of it thereafter...now you assume that I would choose to wait, to inherit my father's wealth...rather than forsake it all for the coachman I love?"

Fontaine watched Knight struggling to contain his emotions.

"I do not care a whit for any of it anymore, Knight," she said. "Any of it…save the livelihood of those who protected me before you came to do it." She exhaled a breath of hope. "I don't think I've cared a whit for it since Mr. Dennis told me I would be disinherited for marrying the man of my choice. I…I only left The Graces in the hope you would…you would…" She brushed a tear from her cheek. "And if you do not want me…I will wait; I will inherit. For there will never be—"

"I love you, Fontaine," he said, reaching out and taking her face in his powerful hands. Fontaine let the tears stream down her cheeks unafraid, unashamed. "I…I never thought any woman could so completely own me," he continued. "You frightened me. I, who feared nothing, feared you…feared for you, at first…feared I would not be able to keep from forcing you into my bed next, when we were playing at lovers. Finally, I feared the loathing I was certain you would feel toward me once you found out who I really was…and how I had deceived you." He shook his head, brushing the tears from her cheeks with his thumbs. "Can you love such a weak man as I am, Fontaine?" he asked, bending and placing his lips to the hollow of her throat. "I would die for you," he whispered, kissing her neck. "I would even play at being a coachman for the rest of my life if it is what would make you marry me."

Fontaine giggled slightly, overcome with relieved joy. Wrapping her arms around his neck as he pulled her against him, she said, "But if I marry you now, I will be penniless. I will have no dowry, no tender or property."

Kissing her mouth lingeringly, Knight smiled and in a low, alluring voice whispered, "You have plenty of tender property, peach."

Gasping, astonished yet delightfully so, she said, "You are a rogue, sir."

"I am," he mumbled, his mouth tasting of hers once more. "And I am yours, lady…your own rogue…Knight."

EPILOGUE

"Oh, Marta," Lady Esperanza Lathan sighed. "What a way you have with luncheon!"

"Yes, Marta! Indeed," Lady Lightender agreed.

"Thank ya, milady…and milady," Marta said, beaming with pride. "I try my best, I do."

Fontaine smiled as she sat under the white picnic pavilion, her full, round belly causing a comfortable position to be elusive. Still, as the tiny life within her moved and kicked, impatient to escape its confines and join the fun of a bright summer's day at The Graces, she was glad for the slight discomfort of her condition.

As she looked around at her friends, all of them, enjoying a lazy picnic on the lawn, she marveled at how wonderful her life was, how blessed. Scarcely more than a year had passed since she and Knight had gone missing from The Graces, and now they had returned as its owners and summer residents. To think of her life before, what her prospects had been, still put a taste of uneasiness in Fontaine's mouth. But Knight would return soon and set the bitterness of the past to rest with one delicious kiss.

It was odd to think on all that had happened. And it had begun with Knight being beaten nearly to death in a darkened alley in winter. The scope of the events to follow was nearly overwhelming—Knight's playing at being Fontaine's lover, his conspiracy to extract her from her aunt's control. And then came their heartache, their loving confessions to one another, and their blessed, beautiful marriage. How Knight had ever convinced Lady Wetherton to sell him The Graces was beyond Fontaine's comprehension. Perhaps it was simply that Lady Wetherton was satisfied with finally inheriting Fontaine's fortune, forfeited when Fontaine married Knight before her nineteenth birthday. Still, the witch had become enraged at discovering Knight's true lineage and the scale of his means. But somehow, whether through pure threatening intimidation or simply the lure of receiving more for the property than it was worth, somehow Knight had saved The Graces from her aunt's loathsome possession. He'd saved it just as he'd saved her. Further, Marta, Daniel, Big William, and many others, having quit her aunt the moment they were sent word of the opportunity to find their home with Fontaine at Lathan Green, had been willing enough yet to leave their new residence for the more familiar surroundings of The Graces.

In all, it seemed a dream come true to be sitting on the lawns of her beloved country estate, surrounded by old friends and others she loved so very dearly. Fontaine marveled at the wonder of it all.

"I must tell Daniel how breathtaking the gardens are this year," Lady Lightender sighed. "What a gift that man has with green and growing things."

"Yes, he does," Lady Lathan added. "I've tried to convince him to winter at Lathan Green this year, to tend my greenhouse…but he is too happy here at The Graces, it seems. And I cannot fault him for it…for it is a beautiful space, Fontaine darling."

"I think so too, Mother," Fontaine said, smiling.

"The sign of a sweet and kind mistress, it is," Lady Lightender said, nodding with approval in Fontaine's direction.

All at once, the calming song of the larks in the trees was stuttered by a sudden boisterous snort from Big William. He lay stretched out on the grass a few feet away, entirely lost in the warmth and peace of a summer nap.

"Oh my!" Lady Lathan giggled. "What a contented noise."

"But wherever is Knight off to?" Lady Lightender asked, shading her face with her hand and searching the green horizon for the rogue.

"I am only just here," Knight said, striding up behind her, bending and kissing her quickly on the cheek. "Come to take my wife away in order to ravish her with much impassioned kissing." Fontaine smiled as Knight took her hand, helping her to her feet. "I've a hearty thirst for peaches, and it is in need of quenching," he said.

"For mercy's sake, Des!" Lady Lathan exclaimed. "You are far too impish yet. Pray try to educate him in a few shreds of propriety here and there, Fontaine. I beg you."

"I've given that up," Fontaine giggled.

"She's never tried, Mother...so do not trust her," Knight chuckled, carefully guiding Fontaine away from the party.

Together they walked along the river, Knight and Fontaine, and Fontaine felt her happiness was complete. Knight was her own, belonged to her only—mind, heart, and soul. She reveled in the simple knowledge she could touch him whenever the urge came upon her, laugh wholeheartedly and comfortably with him, send him into a fit of passion with a simple kiss. And now his child was growing within her body, and the knowledge gave her a pleasure, a joy she could not express in words.

Her thoughts of contentment and unimaginable joy caused her to sigh with satisfaction, and Knight asked, "What is it?"

Fontaine ceased in strolling and turned to look up at him. "You are…you are everything to me, Knight," she told him, her eyes filling with tears.

He smiled, letting his hand caress the firm swell of her stomach. "Am I?" he asked, leaning forward and placing a loving kiss on her forehead.

"You are," she told him, covering his hand with one of her own, "for she is of you too."

"She?" Knight asked, his smile broadening. "How are you so certain it is my daughter you carry?"

Fontaine smiled, gazing into the emerald flash of his eyes. "I've seen her in my dreams of late," she explained.

Knight kissed Fontaine's cheek, letting his lips caress her neck as he whispered, "So have I," into her ear.

"Have you?" she whispered as he turned her, pulling her as tightly against his body as their tender baby would allow.

"I have," he mumbled before tasting her kiss.

"And what is her name?" Fontaine asked, thrilled by the feel of his kisses on her neck.

"Her name is Peaches," he chuckled.

"Peaches?" Fontaine exclaimed, pushing him away playfully. "Why not Apples then?" she giggled.

"Because I prefer peaches," he said, pulling her fully into the power of his embrace.

"Darling," Fontaine said, reaching up and running her fingers through the softness of his hair, "one does not name one's daughter after fruit."

"I see," Knight said. "Then you would prefer we call her Fanny?"

"You are no more than an impish boy today, Desiderio Knight Lathan!" Fontaine giggled. "Now in earnest. What are we to call our daughter?"

Knight's smile faded a bit, but his eyes flashed with emotion. Raising a hand to Fontaine's face, he cupped her cheek in his hand, caressing her lips with his thumb. "In truth, I would beg to call her Pratina…for it is where I found myself…and my love."

Fontaine sighed, awed by his charming tenderness. "Oh, my Knight," she breathed as he held her tightly in his arms, scattering kisses in her hair. "Thank you for rescuing me, for being the Knight of my dreams…for loving me."

"There is only one thing I need for true happiness, my peach," he mumbled, letting his lips gently brush hers as he spoke.

"What might be that one thing?" Fontaine asked, thrilling as the moisture from his lips clung to her own.

"To belong to you and to own you in return. I love you," he mumbled.

In the next moment, Fontaine relished the passion that erupted between them as Knight's mouth captured her own. For as always it spoke to her, confirming to her heart he was hers—her own rogue…the rogue, Knight.

To my hero and inspiration…
Kevin from Heaven!

About the Author

Marcia Lynn McClure's intoxicating succession of novels, novellas, and e-books—including *Shackles of Honor*, *The Windswept Flame*, *A Crimson Frost*, and *The Bewitching of Amoretta Ipswich*—has established her as one of the most favored and engaging authors of true romance. Her unprecedented forte in weaving captivating stories of western, medieval, regency, and contemporary amour void of brusque intimacy has earned her the title "The Queen of Kissing."

Marcia, who was born in Albuquerque, New Mexico, has spent her life intrigued with people, history, love, and romance. A wife, mother, grandmother, family historian, poet, and author, Marcia Lynn McClure spins her tales of splendor for the sake of offering respite through the beauty, mirth, and delight of a worthwhile and wonderful story.

BIBLIOGRAPHY

A Bargained-For Bride

Beneath the Honeysuckle Vine

A Better Reason to Fall in Love

The Bewitching of Amoretta Ipswich

Born for Thorton's Sake

The Chimney Sweep Charm

Christmas Kisses-Three Favorite Holiday Romances

A Cowboy for Christmas

A Crimson Frost

Daydreams

Desert Fire

Divine Deception

Dusty Britches

The Fragrance of her Name

A Good-Lookin' Man

The Haunting of Autumn Lake

The Heavenly Surrender

The Highwayman of Tanglewood

Kiss in the Dark

Kissing Cousins

The Light of the Lovers' Moon

Love Me

The Man of Her Dreams

The McCall Trilogy

Midnight Masquerade

The Object of His Affection

An Old-Fashioned Romance

One Classic Latin Lover, Please

The Pirate Ruse

The Prairie Prince

The Rogue Knight

Romance at the Christmas Tree Lot

Romance in Sleepy Hollow

The Romancing of Evangeline Ipswich

Romantic Vignettes-The Anthology of Premiere Novellas

Romance with a Side of Green Chile

Saphyre Snow

Shackles of Honor

The Secret Bliss of Calliope Ipswich

Sudden Storms

Sweet Cherry Ray

Take a Walk with Me

The Tide of the Mermaid Tears

The Time of Aspen Falls

To Echo the Past

The Touch of Sage

The Trove of the Passion Room

Untethered

The Visions of Ransom Lake

Weathered Too Young

The Whispered Kiss

With a Dreamboat in a Hammock

The Windswept Flame

The Wolf King